KILLING TIME

A JAIL MYSTERY SERIES
BOOK 3

CHRISTINA BOUFIS

CHAPTER 1

Monday 7:30 a.m.

Back to school. Is there any better phrase in the English language? I don't think so. But then again, I'm a teacher. I love the promise early September brings with its return to the classroom. For me, the words conjure the smell of lead from newly sharpened number two pencils. Bright spiral-bound notebooks with their purple, yellow, or green covers, their blank pages just waiting to be filled.

But my students have none of these things. In fact, my students don't have an official start to school. They're in class year-round, with barely a day off for Thanksgiving or Christmas.

They're also not allowed spiral notebooks. The thin, twisty metal could easily be turned into a sharp weapon. Even number two pencils are forbidden.

Instead, I give my students tiny, four-inch golf pencils without erasers—though I doubt any of them have ever been on a golf course. I also have to count the pencils as I hand them out at the beginning and end of class to make sure no one steals one.

Still, I felt a thrill of excitement as I got ready to teach that morning, spending more time than usual with my hair, trying to keep my unruly curls from frizzing. I scooped extra cat food in the bowls of my three cats, which my ex-husband called collectively the Busters, not bothering to differentiate the very different-looking felines.

And finally, I grabbed my jail clearance from my desk along with my lesson plans, and shoved both in a backpack before heading out the door to drive to the San Francisco County Jail.

The new jail, as it was still called despite it being built several years ago, was three miles away from my tiny apartment in North Beach.

My women had a shorter commute. About two hundred steps from the communal pod where they lived, down the hall, to my classroom.

Of course, they didn't wander there on their own. A movement deputy led them single file to my classroom.

They were probably headed to the classroom now. I looked at my Fitbit. Damn. I was going to be late. Traffic snarled through Chinatown. I was stuck behind a bus with a long line of students waiting to board.

But, as my colleague Jazmyn once pointed out, my students would still wait, because, as she asked, "Where they going to go?"

8:15 a.m.

"Morning, Miss P." Erika, one of my favorite students, was always the first to greet me. A large woman, nearly six feet tall, Erika looked even bigger in her bright orange county jail uniform.

But despite her intimidating size, Erika was easygoing, more so than many other women. She always sat up front at the first desk, where she liked to be close to me. And though she wasn't a diligent student, she seemed genuinely interested in whatever lesson I'd planned that day.

Not one of my twenty students called me by my Greek surname, Papadopoulos. Who could blame them? It was a mouthful. When I began teaching nine months earlier, the women immediately shortened it to P. I liked it, and it stuck.

Only Erika took liberties with my first name, too, calling me Char occasionally, short for Charlotte, something only my sister did. And since Helen and I had been estranged, my sister didn't call me much at all.

"Char," Erika said two weeks ago, "I ain't gonna lie. I can't wait to get out of this big ole jail, but I'm gonna miss you."

"Ms. P.," I corrected her. I'd miss Erika too.

Turns out I had little time to.

Like many women, Erika had been released from jail in the middle of the night, something that was common, I'd been shocked to learn when I first started working at the jail.

Less than forty-eight hours later, Erika was rearrested and back in my classroom, with new charges to boot. Assault this time. She'd gotten into a fight with her ex-boyfriend's new girlfriend.

Erika claims she didn't start the fight, and I believe her. But it didn't matter because it was Erika who ended it when she knocked the woman unconscious and sent her to the hospital.

I'd learned the details of Erika's re-arrest from my

colleague Jazmyn, who ran the drug treatment program. Apparently, Erika was blind drunk (alcohol was her drug of choice) and punched the arresting officer, which was unfortunate, and would earn her more jail time.

But Erika didn't seem too concerned about this latest arrest. She smiled at me, waiting for class to begin. Next to Erika at the two-person desk sat Aliyah, a newer student.

Aliyah was hard at work picking at her acne. She'd only been in my classroom a little over a week and, in that time, I'd picked up she had many nervous habits, including gnawing on her cuticles until bright red spots of blood appeared.

Aliyah looked barely out of her teens, and I wondered why she was in jail, but I couldn't ask. What I knew from Aliyah's writing was that she'd had an uncle in jail.

Unfortunately, having relatives in the criminal justice system was a common story.

I glanced at Aliyah and wanted to tell her to stop picking her acne, that it would leave scars, but I wasn't her mother.

Then I glanced down at my roster, which changed every day.

What many people don't understand about jail is that it's a volatile place with a high turnover. Unlike prison, where you're sentenced for a specific time, many jail inmates aren't sure how long they'll be incarcerated. They may be awaiting trial or serving time for a misdemeanor or locked up because they can't afford bail, which was ninety-nine-point-nine percent of my women.

So, as I did each morning, I scanned the women where they sat two to a desk, looking for unfamiliar faces. I didn't see anyone new.

"OK, class," I said. "Let's get started." About half the women looked up.

My students ranged in age from nineteen to forty-something. One gray-haired woman looked closer to fifty or sixty. Most had a grade-school reading level. The majority had never made it past ninth grade.

I'd brought in a poem by Stevie Smith, one of my favorites. I loved all poetry and had minored in twentieth-century poetry during grad school, but I was especially fond of Smith. She'd gotten me through some dark days after my ex left and before I found my calling teaching at the jail.

I handed Erika a stack of photocopies with one of Smith's poems, "Not Waving But Drowning," and she jumped up to distribute them, pleased to be acting as the teacher's pet.

My students were forced to go to class—this was a programs jail, and inmates were required to take part in three rehabilitation programs, such as drug counseling, education, or parenting classes—but I didn't believe in forcing someone to learn. I cajoled. I joked. I worked hard to find literature they might relate to, and all of those things usually worked, eventually.

Besides, I'd found that women were often embarrassed by their lack of literacy skills, so I never forced anyone to read.

But before I could ask for any volunteers, I was drowned out by an ear-piercing siren.

All the women, including myself, immediately put our hands over our ears. The sound was deafening, and I'd never heard it before.

"What's that?" I mouthed to Erika.

Erika shook her head that she didn't know.

After a minute, in which I was sure at least one of my eardrums had burst, the air horn siren stopped.

"Shelter in place!" a deputy's voice barked over the PA system.

Was it an earthquake? I hadn't felt any shaking. And the jail, especially since it was so new, must be earthquake proof.

I glanced at the back wall of the classroom, which was made of reinforced glass, allowing anyone in the hallway to see what we were doing. Two deputies were standing outside. One stuck his head in and shouted for us to get under the desks.

"What's going on?" I asked.

He didn't answer, just shook his head at me.

Whatever was happening, it wasn't an earthquake.

"Go under your desks, ladies," I said more calmly than I felt.

"I'm not gettin' on the floor. That shit is nasty," Erika said. I looked at the deputy. He was a young corrections officer, which was good news for Erika.

If he'd been more experienced, he probably would have written her up for two rules violations. One for cursing. Another for not obeying his direct order.

But I needed to intervene.

"Come on," I said. "Let's play it safe and do what we need to." I sat under Erika and Aliyah's desk on the industrial carpet, which was no doubt dirty.

The other women moaned and complained, but everyone eventually complied. Something serious and unprecedented was going on, and the women, who I'd found to be emotionally astute, knew it.

After the women were situated, I told them I'd be right back, and got up. Their eyes followed me as I went out into the hallway, where the two deputies were stationed.

"What's happening?" I asked again.

The other deputy was an older man with short, cropped hair graying at the sides. I recognized him, but he wasn't our typical movement deputy. He had several more chevrons on his uniform. Perhaps he was a sergeant or a captain—I could never remember the hierarchy at the jail, though my colleague and friend Deputy Cunningham had explained the ranks to me several times.

"You're supposed to be sheltering in place," the older deputy said. His name badge read Chisholm.

"Sergeant Chisholm," I began. I must have gotten his rank correct, as he didn't correct me. "I need to tell my students something—how long we're supposed to be sheltering in place, what we're sheltering from, why we're—"

"You don't need to tell them anything," he interrupted. "There's a lockdown order and you will follow it."

My back practically arched in anger. "I'm not going to blindly follow an order from you—"

"There's a suicide bomber in the lobby." His voice was terse. "Now stay with your students and shelter in place."

CHAPTER 2

Ellie Forzano planned on dropping her two sons right in front of Oakland High School, but when she slowed the car, her older son shouted at her to keep going.

"You can't let us out here," Jack, a junior, said. He shifted his six-foot frame lower into the passenger seat. "It's so lame that I don't have my own car."

It was on the tip of Ellie's tongue to tell Jack he should be grateful he didn't have to take the bus and grateful as well that he had a mother who would be late for her own job so she could take him to school the first day of class.

What was more infuriating was that Jack should know better. Money had been tight since her husband, Ben, was laid off from his nonprofit a year ago. Ben hadn't found steady work since. Jack must have noticed that they didn't eat out anymore. Even takeout burritos were a rare treat.

But Ellie bit her tongue and said nothing. She was

excited—and immensely relieved—that summer was over and her boys were back at school. No more trying to find camps that neither one would go to, preferring, as they did, to sleep late and play video games all day. She wouldn't let her ungrateful oldest child take away her joy and relief that they were finally back in school.

Jack turned his head away from the hordes of students milling about on the sparse brown lawn of the school grounds and motioned for Ellie to keep driving.

The high school was the largest public school in Oakland, nearly the size of two airplane hangars. It had massive Greek columns flanking the front of the school and three different entrances, with an enormous set of steps leading up to the main door.

Ellie thought it highly unlikely that the groups of teenagers hanging around outside would give them a second thought, but she did as Jack asked and pulled into a bus stop a block away.

"Better?" she asked sarcastically.

Jack grunted and got out of the car, swinging his backpack over one shoulder. He didn't bother saying thank you or goodbye. She was tempted to get out of the car and shout, "You're welcome" at him in her best sarcastic tone, but she refrained. She'd talk to him later about his attitude.

Max, her younger son, the easy-going one, didn't follow his brother or even unclip his seatbelt. Instead, he looked down at the car floor.

Ellie turned off the ignition and opened the windows. She knew this might take a while.

"Everything alright?"

Ellie knew it wasn't, yet she had to ask.

Max shrugged and fiddled with the straps of his backpack. Ellie's heart constricted for her youngest, her baby. She would give her right arm and probably even her left as well if she could soothe his anxiety.

While Jack was outgoing, Max was the opposite—introverted. Though he'd been an easy baby and a quiet toddler, perhaps he'd been too easy? His teachers praised his composure. But it was only recently that Ellie and Ben had learned Max struggled with a deep well of anxiety, something he tried hard to hide from others.

Ellie felt like the worst mother in the world. She'd mistaken Max's placid surface for contentment when it was anything but.

She only learned of it this summer when Max's first girlfriend dumped him after a week. "He wasn't that interesting or fun to hang out with," she'd blasted on social media.

Ellie's first emotion was white-hot fury. She wanted to call this teen and yell at her. How dare she hurt her son like that? How dare she call Max boring?

But what had emerged from this heartbreak was that Max confessed he'd been silently struggling with social anxiety for years. She and Ben had missed it.

The pit in Ellie's stomach grew. She knew the massive size of the school was overwhelming for Max. And of course, there was the possibility of running into his short-lived ex-girlfriend.

If they'd had money, she would send him to a small private high school. He'd thrive there. Many times, she sat at her desk at work, scanning private school websites, looking for scholarships or ways to make the cost affordable. It wasn't. Private high school tuition in the Bay Area was higher than that at most colleges. They'd never be able to afford it. Even at half price.

"It'll probably go better than you think," Ellie said gently.

Max shook his head.

Ellie resisted the urge to reach over the seat and move the hair obscuring Max's downcast eyes. She resisted the urge to scoop him up and hold him tight and tell him everything would be alright. She knew it might not be. How had she produced two sons so entirely different? One with enough self-esteem for them both? The other struggling to get out of the car?

"Hey, Max." A voice startled them both.

"Hey, Nate." Max smiled when one of his few friends stuck his head in the open passenger seat window.

"You coming?" Nate asked.

Max grabbed his backpack and tried to leave the car, then realized he was still buckled in. He gave a little laugh, a sound that Ellie hadn't heard in a long while.

"Thanks, Mom," Max said. Ellie watched with relief as he walked off with Nathan, a kid he'd known since middle school.

Ellie glanced at her reflection in the rearview mirror and saw more wrinkles around her blue eyes and gray in her blond hair. She'd aged this summer.

She sighed and started the car, but before she could pull away from the curb, her phone buzzed, loud and insistent. She rummaged around in her bag, which Jack had pushed onto the passenger-side floor until she found it.

"Forzano?" It was Bates McGuire, her editor. He only called her by her last name when he was under pressure.

"Where are you?"

"I'm on my way in. Bridge is backed up." This was not technically a lie. Though she was still a few miles away from the Bay Bridge, she could guarantee the metering lights would be on, slowing traffic to a standstill.

"Don't you have a source inside the jail?"

Ellie was surprised by the question. She didn't remember telling Bates about Charlotte. And the source wasn't just a source anymore; she was a friend.

"Yeah, why?"

"Well, see if you can reach her."

"Why? What's going on?"

"Suicide bomber at the jail. It's on lockdown. Hall of Justice too. It's a circus. Media's being kept away. I want this story. Bring it to me." Then he hung up.

Ellie didn't move but sat there staring at her phone.

Her first thought was not of the story but of Charlotte. She would be at the jail now, teaching. With a suicide bomber somewhere inside the jail.

A blast from a bus horn behind her caused Ellie to jump.

She quickly pulled away from the curb, waving an apology to the bus driver. Then she tapped on Charlotte's name in her list of favorites. The call went straight to voicemail. That didn't necessarily mean anything. She knew cell phones weren't allowed upstairs in the jail classroom. She hung up. Then, she tried again and heard the familiar sound of Charlotte's cheerful voice on the message. Ellie tried to keep her voice steady as she left a message asking her friend to call her back.

As she'd predicted, traffic on the Bay Bridge was crawling. As she inched along, she wondered who'd want to bomb a jail? A terrorist? A former inmate? An activist protesting incarceration? As a crime reporter for the *San Francisco Herald* for over a decade, Ellie could think of lots of reasons someone might have a beef with the criminal justice system, but why threaten to kill hundreds of inmates and staff?

When the traffic sped up for no apparent reason, Ellie pressed down on the accelerator. Her worries about Max receded into the background, replaced by fear for Charlotte and everyone at the jail.

CHAPTER 3

8:40 a.m.

I'd never been in such close physical proximity to my students. Erika and I were crammed under the desk, our knees touching. Aliyah was on the other side of me, scrunched as closely as she could by my side. Since she'd been in the jail, Aliyah had stuck close to me in the classroom, but never this close. The harsh industrial scent of laundry detergent from my student's uniforms, and their body odors, was pungent.

"Damn, Char," Erika said, taking advantage of our intimate circumstances to call me by my first name. "I'm starving. How long they gonna keep us here?"

"I don't know." I shook my head, keenly aware that I knew more than my students about the cause of the lockdown.

I was starting to feel a little claustrophobic, hemmed in my Erika on one side, and Aliyah on the other, who was using her time to bite her nails.

It had been twenty minutes since the alarm blared and

we were told to take cover. Twenty minutes since I found out there was a suicide bomber. It felt like twenty hours.

I pictured what might be going on in the lobby. Anyone could enter the jail. And anyone did. The front lobby door wasn't locked, at least during business hours.

Inside, the lobby was lined with green and maroon high-backed sofas that looked more Alice in Wonderland than county jail. They were an expensive purchase of taxpayer money and had earned the jail the nickname, The Glamour Slammer, though the moniker was fading from memory.

When I'd asked her about it, Sheriff O'Connor told me the jail was required by law to spend a certain amount of money on public art. In her book, the sofas counted. "Why shouldn't inmates' families have somewhere comfortable to sit?" she'd asked.

In addition to the sofas, a deputy was stationed behind a large metal desk. On top of the desk was a thick binder with a blue cover that contained a daily printout listing all the inmates currently housed at one of the three San Francisco County jails.

My office, the one I shared with Jazmyn, was just off the lobby through a locked door.

Thinking about Jazmyn, my heart beat faster. Was she in the office? I hadn't seen her this morning as I'd dropped my backpack and rushed upstairs.

If Jazmyn was in our office, then there was no way for her to get out except through the lobby—which would put her directly in the path of the bomber. Jazmyn has a wife and four kids.

Then there was Will, a new teacher I'd just hired. Over the summer, I'd been promoted to help lead a new charter school at the jail, which meant hiring additional teachers for subjects I didn't teach, like math and science.

But we'd had a hard time finding qualified instructors who wanted to work for little money.

Today was Will's official start. He was an older man who'd retrained as a teacher. Was he downstairs too, just a wall separating him from the suicide bomber?

Then I also remembered who was manning the desk this morning. Cunningham. My heart caught in my throat. Deputy Cunningham was the women's favorite and mine too. Most of the other deputies ignored me, but not Cunningham. She was a friend. Had the bomber taken her hostage?

Weren't we *all* hostages? How come we hadn't been evacuated? What exactly was the plan? Where were the police?

I had to turn my head away from Erika when I thought about the police because I suddenly pictured a very handsome, dark-haired homicide detective, Mark Ryan, and my face felt flushed. Since we'd met last April when I'd found my landlord murdered, he's never been far from my thoughts.

Ryan, as everyone calls him, and I have developed a friendship with a strong undercurrent of electricity. Though we've kissed passionately more than once, we've never fully acted on our desire, mostly because Ryan has a beautiful, smart girlfriend, and I find three makes an awkward number in a relationship.

Still, that didn't stop me from fantasizing about Ryan.

Was Ryan thinking about me and worrying about my safety? I shook my head to dislodge the self-centered thought. I wasn't the only one who would die if the bomber succeeded.

Next to me, Aliyah picked at the hem of her orange sweatpants.

"What's happening, Ms. P.?" She looked more nervous than usual, and rightly so.

"There's a disturbance in the lobby," I said, trying to be as evasive as possible. "They're dealing with it."

There was no sense sharing the information there was a suicide bomber downstairs. And yet, I wondered, as I looked into Aliyah's dark brown eyes full of worry, didn't the women have a right to know? If the unthinkable happened and the bomber succeeded, was it fair to keep the knowledge of a bomber to myself as we were all blasted to pieces?

On the other hand, if I did tell the women, there'd probably be a riot as they all charged out of the classroom. They'd insist on using the pay phone to call loved ones. Maybe that's what we all should be doing?

I violated a jail rule about not touching inmates as I put my hand over Aliyah's and told her it would be alright. A lie, I thought.

"I'll be right back," I told her, squeezing her hand. Still, Aliyah gave a small cry as I scooched out from under the desk. She even put her thin hand out to try to stop me. In the short time I'd known her, she seemed to imprint on me like a duckling.

I could see the younger deputy was still in the hallway. Chisholm had gone. Was that a good or bad sign?

"Miss P., what are you doing?" Leticia, one of my students, hissed at me as I walked towards the door.

Leticia was one of the oldest students. Her thick braids were streaked with gray, and she was missing quite a few front teeth, as well as the bottom part of an earlobe. Her hard life was written in every wrinkle and scar on her face. Yet despite her rough looks, Leticia was a mother hen, maternal towards all the women, including me.

"It's OK," I said. Leticia shook her head.

I went into the hallway and closed the door gently behind me.

"You need to get back in the classroom." The order came out more as a suggestion than a command. I felt a stab of pity for this young deputy, who seemed as nervous as Aliyah.

I looked at his name tag.

"What can I tell the women, Deputy Lopez? They're asking what's going on. And I can't just say nothing."

"Tell them we wait until we're told what to do."

"Are we going to be evacuated?"

The younger deputy shifted his feet and stepped back awkwardly. "We wait for orders."

"Got it," I said. "And when do you think we'll get them?"

Lopez started to shrug, then said, "When we get orders, you'll know." His voice tried and failed to be commanding. "You have to get back in the classroom."

I sighed and did as Lopez suggested. I went back inside the classroom.

The women looked up at me from under their desks.

"No news," I said. "We just have to wait."

"Damn, Ms. P. They can't do that. It's against our civil rights." Erika led the chorus and others soon joined in about their rights. This was one of my women's favorite complaints. Though I wasn't sure how being locked down in a classroom violated any right, other than the right to know what was happening, I didn't respond.

But I needed to do something. So, I stood in front of the classroom and told everyone we were going to continue with the lesson. I read Smith's poem aloud.

It was about a man who had swum too far from the shore. Bystanders didn't hear him calling for help. They'd mistaken his actions. The man hadn't been waving at them, but drowning.

CHAPTER 4

8:35 a.m.

Deputy Cunningham kept her eyes on the man from the moment she'd looked up and seen him spidering across the lobby. Even before her brain fully registered the man in the black balaclava, she'd sensed a nervous, dangerous energy about him and reached for her pepper spray.

But before she could release it from her utility belt, the man spoke to her.

"Don't," he said, pushing aside his jacket with one hand to reveal a row of red cylindrical explosives with several wires taped to them. In his right hand, the man gripped what looked like an older iPhone with his finger poised over a button.

"Now, do exactly what I say. Pick up your radio."

Cunningham slowly removed her walkie-talkie and held it up in the air.

"What's your name?"

He shook his head.

"OK," she said, keeping her voice casual. "I'm Deputy Cunningham." She looked into the man's dark brown eyes, visible through his mask. It was important to keep eye contact, though the man's eyes were darting around the lobby.

Cunningham slowly came from behind her desk, holding her radio with one hand to show she was complying.

"Tell them to lock down the jail. Now."

Cunningham nodded. Then she glanced around the lobby. It was empty. Just minutes before the man came in, she'd kicked out an unhoused couple, Fred and Ethel, as she called them. The two came in every morning to wash up in the bathrooms. Sometimes Cunningham let them sleep on the sofas. But today they were noisier than usual. And Fred reeked of alcohol. So she told them it was a nice day, and they needed to sleep it off somewhere else. Now she was glad she did.

But just off the jail lobby was a suite of staff offices. She glanced to her right, where behind a wall sat how many civilians? At least four. Tony Mendoza had left for a meeting at City Hall. She'd seen Charlotte rush upstairs to teach. That left Jazmyn, the new teacher, and two admins. All of whom would be dead or severely injured if the bomb detonated.

"Lock it down. Now. Or we end it here." The man waved the iPhone with his finger over the detonator.

"Alright." Cunningham picked up her radio.

"We have a situation in the lobby," she said. "There is a man with a device. A bomb. It has not been activated. I repeat it has not been activated. He demands we lock down the jail now."

"Uh, Cunningham. Roger that."

"Tell them no evacuations," the bomber said.

Cunningham relayed the message. Then she instinctively looked up at one of the surveillance cameras in the lobby. No doubt the control room was watching them and verifying everything she said.

When the bomber saw her gaze, he reached into his jacket pocket with his free hand.

"Do it. All of them." He held out a can of black spray paint and motioned to the two other surveillance cameras.

How did he know where the cameras were?

Cunningham moved around the lobby, spray-painting the cameras. She was tall enough so that she could aim the nozzle and black out the lenses.

Both Cunningham and the bomber turned to look at the lobby front door. The automatic lock clicked shut. As did the one leading to the suite of offices. They were complying, so far, with the bomber's demands.

The radio sprang to life, and a voice she recognized, but rarely heard, her captain, Jay Park, called for her.

"Tell them. Tell them again no evacuations," the bomber said. "Every exit is wired. I'll blow them up anyone tries to move."

Cunningham picked up her radio. "No evacuations. I repeat. There are more bombs at the exits. No one is to be evacuated."

"Roger that, Deputy. Can we speak to the man in the lobby?" Captain Park said.

The bomber shook his head no.

"Put the radio on the desk." The man pointed to the metal desk Cunningham had been sitting behind just a few minutes ago when the only thing on her mind was another cup of coffee and a leftover Danish.

Now, all thoughts except one had vanished from her

mind. She needed to figure out how to calm the man down and disarm him. He was on the shorter side, about five feet seven. Cunningham herself was over six feet tall. She could easily have taken him—if he hadn't been wired with explosives.

What did he want with the jail?

"Mr....?" Cunningham let her voice trail off.

He shook his head no.

"What can I do for you?" she asked.

"You've done enough. All of you."

So, the man must have been an inmate—or had a loved one incarcerated. Even though she worked for the Sheriff's Department, Cunningham could think of many reasons a bomber might want to blow up the jail. Mental health services were almost nonexistent. Even the rehabilitation programs only scratched the surface of the vast needs of inmates, who were mostly poor people of color.

Yes, most of them had committed a crime, some violent, most misdemeanors. And while she didn't excuse them, Cunningham gave inmates the benefit of the doubt—most hadn't been sentenced or convicted, and she believed in treating people with respect. They were guests of the San Francisco correctional facility until they were sentenced and moved on to prison or were released.

Most of her colleagues in corrections didn't agree with her views.

"I understand," Cunningham told the bomber, softly.

The sound of sirens filtered in through the thick cement of the jail.

"Call and tell them to keep everyone back from the jail." The bomber shifted on his feet.

Cunningham nodded, picked up the radio, and told her colleagues to keep a large perimeter around the jail.

The bomber nodded, and Cunningham noticed he seemed to relax.

"Hey, I think I know you." Cunningham took a gamble. Indeed, the man's voice did sound familiar.

He had no trace of an accent, but his voice was distinctively higher pitched, and she guessed it was not just from nervousness. While most deputies found the women much harder than the men to oversee, Cunningham preferred to work in the women's pods. But she'd rotated through the men's pods as well and had a feeling she'd seen this guy before.

Tread carefully, a voice in her head told her. Not only was her own life in danger, but the lives of everyone at the jail.

A picture of Cunningham's elderly mother flashed through her mind. She worked every overtime shift and commuted over an hour each way to pay for 24/7 care for her mother with dementia. What would happen to her mom if she were killed?

The man said nothing.

"I know it can suck in here. The food especially. Am I right?" Cunningham kept her voice light, friendly.

She'd had little formal training in hostage negotiation, but she had empathy, and maybe that was enough?

Still, the man said nothing. But he relaxed his right hand —the one that hovered over the button, just a bit. She imagined herself lunging for the detonator. The distance between them was only about four feet. The gamble was too great. He'd have pressed the button and blown them both up before she could get to him.

"And you don't know how long you're gonna be in here, right?" Cunningham continued her monologue. "You gotta follow all the rules. Line up for count when we tell you to. Eat when we tell you to. Do this. Do that. Am I right?"

"Shut up," the man said. "It's not going to work," the man said. "It's too late for all that. I'm not playing your game."

"I'm not playing no game." Cunningham raised her hands as if in surrender. "I don't know what your experience was like here. All I'm saying is you have a right to have some legitimate beef with this place. You probably weren't even sentenced yet when you came here. And you were doing time for something you may or may not have done."

The man exhaled, and Cunningham took that as a sign to continue. She was on the right track. He must have been a former inmate.

"And then once you get released, where you gonna go? What you going to do? You got a record and it's not easy getting a job after that. Girlfriend might have left you. Family—if you're lucky enough to have them—no longer support you. Odds are even more stacked against you then before you came into the system. Am I right?"

Cunningham tried again. "What can I call you?"

The man gave a short laugh and then began to rattle off a series of numbers in a harsh staccato voice. Cunningham immediately recognized the string of numerals as a jail ID number. She'd been right. She wished she could write it down, but the bomber talked too fast, and she only got the first new numbers.

Just then, a voice blared through the walkie-talkie.

"Cunningham. Come in."

The man took a step backwards. Cunningham held her breath, waiting for an explosion.

It didn't happen. She didn't answer the call. Or move towards the radio. Instead, she raised her hands and said, "Look. I'm really sorry about what happened to you here. I really am," Cunningham said, her voice softer. "I just think we can work this out a different way."

The man shook his head no.

"Now I have to get this." Cunningham looked at the radio. "You want to talk? Let them know about your experience here?"

"You talk." He backed up, further away from Cunningham. "You tell them if anyone tries to come in, or they start evacuating, bombs are going off."

Cunningham nodded. She pressed the talk button.

"Cunningham here." Then she repeated the bomber's demands to keep the jail locked down.

She looked at the bomber. "You got anything you want to add Mr. Four, zero, six...?" Cunningham started to repeat the numbers she'd heard.

"You stop that," he said, cutting her off and coming closer, his finger poised above the detonator.

"You tell them I want to go up to D pod. You're gonna take me there. You hear? Or we both gone down."

Cunningham nodded to calm the man down. What did he want with D pod? Was he once housed there? One thing she knew for sure, the bomber was never leaving the lobby.

CHAPTER 5

9:15 a.m.

Ellie couldn't get within half a mile of the jail. She was turned away at Fifth and Harrison Street, two long blocks away. Squad cars had blocked all the intersections, red and blue lights flashing.

As instructed, Ellie turned left—or tried to—and was instantly caught in gridlock.

"Damn!" She hit the steering wheel in frustration. In doing so, she momentarily lifted her foot off the brake and rolled into the car in front of her.

"Fuck's sake," Ellie said. She watched as a man got out of the car she hit cursing and waving in her direction.

"You hit my new Honda," he said.

Ellie looked at the car in front of her. True, it was a gray Honda of some type, but it didn't look all that new. She was driving a Honda as well, a twenty-year-old CR-V they'd inherited from Ben's parents.

"I'm sorry. I didn't hit you exactly," Ellie said.

"You did. You hit my new Honda." The man gesticulated wildly towards his car.

Ellie fished in her purse for her license and insurance.

Then, she got out of her car and inspected both bumpers. Not a scratch on either car as far as she could tell. She ignored the man, who kept repeating that she'd hit his new car while she snapped photos with her phone.

Then she walked towards the intersection to see if she could get a better look down Harrison Street to see if she could make out what might be happening at the jail.

"What are you doing? You can't just walk away. I'm reporting this," the man shouted after her.

"Be my guest," Ellie said over her shoulder.

She got back in her car and put her license and insurance away.

Ellie looked up. Above the noise of horns sounded by impatient drivers and the shouts of police telling everyone to move away, she heard the distinctive *thwack*, *thwack*, *thwack* of a helicopter. Was it going to land on the Hall of Justice? She wasn't sure the Hall had a helipad, and considering the building was adjacent to the jail, she doubted it would take the chance.

No, it was a news helicopter reading KTXV in large, unmistakable letters. That was fast, she thought. But she wasn't surprised at the media leak.

Bates had sources at the jail, but so did other outlets. And while he wanted the story, this wasn't a story to Ellie. She didn't care who scooped her. She said a silent prayer that Charlotte and everyone in the jail had been evacuated to safety.

She turned to see the man she'd hit trying to flag down a policeman to report the accident. Fortunately, he wasn't having any luck.

Then he put his hand on the back of his neck and motioned to Ellie.

"You'll be hearing from my lawyer," he shouted at her.

"Fine. Whatever," Ellie said.

How long was the gridlock going to last? Ellie considered abandoning her car and getting out and walking. But somehow the number of uniformed police mushroomed before her. They were erecting barriers and now directing pedestrians away from the sidewalk blockades.

Ellie was trapped. Out of frustration and fear, she took out her phone and tapped on Charlotte's name again. It went to voicemail. Then she scrolled through her contacts until she got to Detective Ryan's name. His phone too went to voicemail. Ellie left a message.

She'd known Detective Mark Ryan for years. He'd always been fair with her, and she with him. He'd answered her questions when he could and kept silent when he couldn't.

Through Charlotte, she'd gotten to know Ryan more on a personal level. Charlotte was attracted to the handsome detective, and they'd had many discussions about him, where Charlotte discreetly tried to ask for information.

Ellie had also met Ryan's girlfriend, Olivia, at several city functions. Olivia was from a wealthy family and a somewhat minor celebrity. Besides her reputation as a fierce attorney for many high-powered clients, Olivia was known for her beauty. Yet Ellie found Olivia cold, unlike Charlotte, who was fiery and whose passion and fierce loyalty to her friends and students radiated off of her.

The first time she invited Charlotte to her house for dinner, even her sons had looked up from their phones and shown interest in their guest. They'd peppered her with questions about the jail.

"Aren't you scared in there?" Max asked.

"Do you teach murderers?" Leave it to Jake to ask that question.

Charlotte had laughed. "No and yes," she'd answered, then described what it was like to work in a jail where her students lived in pods rather than in cells with bars.

As for murderers, yes, she had those too, but she explained that she wasn't allowed to ask personal questions —and that most inmates in jail had not been tried or convicted and were presumed innocent.

Ben was also intrigued by Charlotte. Since he'd lost his job last year and hadn't been able to find a new one, he'd been depressed. Visits with Charlotte seemed to buoy him up for a while and make him more optimistic.

Ellie's phone buzzed, and she jumped.

"Ellie. Have you heard from Charlotte?" There was no introduction, only an edge of hopefulness in Ryan's voice.

"No. I tried her. She must be teaching."

"Yeah."

"What's going on, Ryan? Who is this bomber and what does he want? Are they evacuating everyone?"

There was a slight pause.

"Off the record, Ryan," Ellie added.

"The Sheriff's Department is setting up a Unified Command Center. ATF is on its way. We're finding a hostage negotiator..."

"There are hostages?" Ellie cut him off.

"The entire jail is a hostage situation."

"They didn't evacuate?"

"Not yet." Ryan exhaled loudly. "They can't yet. It's complicated."

"What do you mean 'it's complicated'? How come everyone is still inside? Where's the bomber?"

"He's in the lobby."

Ellie heard voices in the background.

"Look, Ellie, I have to go. Just let me know if you hear from Charlotte."

"I will," she promised.

"And Ellie," Ryan paused, "If you're thinking of coming near the jail, don't. Get as far away as you can."

CHAPTER 6

After trying to force a lesson that no one was interested in, I was about to give up. Only a few of the women were paying attention anyway. And though I couldn't have known what this day would bring, I regretted my choice of a poem about dying. We were all drowning and didn't know it—or my women didn't, and I was growing increasingly uncomfortable keeping them in the dark.

I was glad when Erika distracted us.

"Why's she called Stevie? She trans?"

"Good question." I explained Stevie was a childhood nickname, and the poet's given name was Florence Margaret Smith.

"Damn. That's a mouthful," Erika said.

That was all it took to derail the lesson from the poetry to the poet. Another student jumped in, defending the name Stevie and deciding that the poet must be non-binary like them. The discussion then veered sharply towards gender identity and how there should be a pod just for people who don't identify as male or female—something I had wondered about.

Usually I steered the discussion back to the text, but this time I let the conversation wash over me, glad the women were talkative and needed no input from me. I was exhausted and wired at the same time.

After a few more minutes, the discussion petered out, and my students went back to trying to sleep or cuddle with each other under their desks. Though physical contact between inmates was strictly forbidden, I didn't have the heart to tell the women to separate under the circumstances.

Erika stood up. "Damn. Char. I'm not hiding out under there no more. I want to go back to the pod. I'm starving."

Her rebellion was contagious. Some of my other students also scooted out from under their desks and stood up, looking antsy. I didn't think I could contain them much longer.

"How about we stretch for a bit?" I brought my arms over my head and stretched toward the ceiling, asking the women to do the same.

Erika looked at me as if I'd lost my mind. "What's this now, PE?"

At least she got a laugh from some of the other women.

I stretched to the right and then to the left, leading by example.

Erika and some of the others, including Aliyah and Leticia, my youngest and oldest students, joined in too. I wondered if Deputy Lopez was watching and what he must think of this latest lesson plan.

Then my students took it one step further, shaking their hips and dancing around in their bright orange sweatshirts and sweatpants. One woman with a lovely voice started rapping—whether it was her own song or another artist's, I didn't know. Erika did a drumbeat on the desk.

We were dangerously close to being out of control.

Poor Lopez was out of his depth if he thought about coming in and trying to restore order.

But as quickly as the energy had energized the women, it dissipated. Moods spread through the jail like wildfire, and this one was quickly turning darker.

Time was ticking. And still, we were on lockdown.

"This is stupid," one woman said. "What are we waiting for?"

"They can't keep us here like this."

I agreed. I strode through the classroom and stuck my head out into the hallway.

"Any news?" My voice was louder than I had intended.

Lopez shook his head no.

"It's been almost an hour, right? You'd think they'd have a plan."

Just then, Lopez's radio crackled. The deputy released it from his utility belt, turned away from me, and stepped down the hall before he pressed the button.

I heard a bunch of static, some codes, which didn't make sense to me, and then a "Roger that," from Lopez. He clipped his radio back onto his belt and walked towards me.

"Any update?" I asked.

"No. Evacuation's on hold." Deputy Lopez said.

"Why?"

"Bomb squad is checking the exits. Bomber says they're wired. Look, get back in the classroom," Lopez said, knowing he'd revealed too much.

As I stood with my hand on the doorknob, I realized just

how quiet the classroom had become. The women had been listening.

"There's a bomber!" Erika screamed.

What happened next was equally explosive. The women pushed each other as they stormed towards the door and out into the hallway. Chairs were overturned. Women shouted. Someone screamed. I tried to stand firm but was swept away by the tide of women.

Lopez was no match for my students, either.

Though he shouted at them to get back in the classroom, the women started running down the hallway back towards the communal pod where they lived.

Just then, Sergeant Chisholm rounded the corner.

He stood firm in his khaki uniform, blocking the hallway. Then he reached for his baton.

"There's no need for that," I said, rushing past my students, who were now frozen in place.

"What's happening?" Erika asked Chisholm directly.

The hallway was suddenly silent.

"We have a right to know what's going on," I said.

"We're still in a lockdown situation," the sergeant said.

"Why can't we get out of here?" Erika asked.

Chisholm hesitated, then said, "There's no evacuation plan right now."

"Nobody give a damn about us," Erika said. The women murmured their agreement.

I had to agree with her.

CHAPTER 7

9:35 a.m.

When the car in front of her, the one she'd hit, though 'hit' really was too strong a word, started to move, Ellie finally made a right turn away from the jail and drove toward the Embarcadero. She'd have to go west along the waterfront and then in a round-about way head back up Market Street, hoping that the thoroughfare would be open as it was several long blocks from the jail.

Traffic crawled, and horns blasted from hot-tempered drivers as everyone tried to navigate the gridlock.

Ellie glanced at her phone. How was it possible that just two hours ago she was dropping off her boys at Oakland High? She had a brief pang realizing she hadn't thought about Max since earlier this morning. She wondered if he was all right.

As Ellie inched up Market Street, she was keenly aware of how much time was ticking by. Every red light, every pedestrian with a death wish who crossed in front of her, slowed her down.

She couldn't make a left-hand turn on Market and again had to detour right to finally make a left and head down south of Market Street in the direction of the jail, but several blocks from it.

She was closer to her office at the Herald and decided to pull into the underground parking lot. Though Bates wanted a story, she wanted to find out what was happening at the jail and whether Charlotte had been evacuated safely. She'd park and walk as close as she could get.

Before she got out of her car, she texted Max.

How's it going?

This was shorthand for *How are you feeling? Are you alright? Feeling anxious?*

She watched as three dots appeared to show Max was typing. But no text appeared.

Ellie started texting again. She wanted to ask if he'd run into Bella, his ex-girlfriend, or if he had classes with any of his friends. Then she backspaced, deleting what she'd written.

"He'll figure it out on his own," Ben had suggested when she confessed last night how worried she was about Max at the new high school. "Maybe you should give him the chance."

Though a large part of her wanted to bite Ben's head off and tell him he should be equally worried about their son, she didn't. Fighting before going to bed only led to insomnia. And maybe Ben was right. Maybe she hovered too much.

Ellie put her phone in her purse and hurried out of the garage and into the bright light of an autumn San Francisco day.

Ellie was able to walk down Bryant to Ninth Street. But she was prevented from going any further by hordes of squad cars, barricades, and police in riot gear, who held a firm line and told pedestrians to clear the area.

Ellie had no such intention. She squeezed her way through the crowd, apologizing as she did so. She needed to get closer. Maybe she could see something—like hundreds of inmates wearing orange being led away from the jail.

She saw nothing like that.

Instead, peering down Bryant Street, she saw only flashing red and blue lights of police and rescue vehicles and barricades everywhere.

Ellie's phone buzzed in her purse. Could it be Charlotte? She frantically fished her phone out from the bottom of her purse, where it always concealed itself, cursing as she did so.

I think I'm gonna go home.

Oh, no. Ellie read the text from Max, and her heart literally hurt. She paused a second before typing back. *What's up?*

Maybe he wasn't feeling well. Did he have a stomachache, or was he coming down with a cold?

Ellie waited for Max to reply. He didn't.

Fuck this about figuring it out himself. Ellie pressed call.

"Hullo." Max's voice was barely audible.

"Hey there." Ellie tried to keep her voice upbeat.

Just then, a police officer with a bullhorn shouted for people to stand back and leave the area.

"Where are you?" Max asked.

"I'm uh, near the office." Not technically a lie, but she was a brisk ten-minute walk away from the *Herald*'s offices.

"What's happening? I hear a lot of noise."

All around her, people were moving, pushing past, some muttering about defunding the police.

"There's an incident at the jail," Ellie said at last. She decided to be honest. "There's a bomb threat and—"

"Mom. You're not near there, are you?"

"Oh no, sweetheart. I'm far away from the jail."

"Is Charlotte OK?"

Ellie paused. "As far as we know. But look, don't worry. There are a lot of police and first responders working to de-escalate the situation."

"That doesn't sound good."

"Now what's this about going home?" Ellie asked.

"I'm just not feeling it today," Max said. "I hate this school. I don't have any friends here—"

"What about Nate?"

"Yeah. I don't have any classes with him."

"I see." Ellie desperately wanted to say the right thing, to give her son some motherly advice that would work. "It's only the first day, sweetheart. Can you give stick it out and see how you feel by the end of the day. I know the first day can be overwhelming and—"

"Move back!" Uniformed police with their shields raised were advancing on the onlookers, pushing spectators back.

"Mom?"

"Look, I should go. But promise me you'll stay today at school and we can talk about it later?"

"Yeah, I guess so."

"Did you eat lunch?"

"It's not even lunch time."

"Why don't you eat something? You'll feel better. Do you have a Clif bar?"

"Move! Now!" The formidable line of police stood right before Ellie, reminding her of Stormtroopers in *Star Wars*.

"I've got to go. Love you. Bye."

Ellie hung up, her heart a fist in her chest. Then she turned around and walked a few steps away from the scene.

Her phone buzzed again.

"Ellie, what have you got?" Bates asked without any preliminaries.

"I'm here close to Ninth and Bryant at the police barricade. But Bates, I've got to go. The police are—"

"Call me when you have something."

Don't worry about me, Ellie said out loud after Bates hung up.

Ellie moved with the swarm of people away from the direction of the jail. Though she didn't like retreating, it was impossible to see anything anyway.

As she walked, she tried not to feel like a failure—failing as a mother to help her anxious son, failing as a journalist to get the story or even get close to the action, failing as a friend to help Charlotte. Then she pushed the self-pity aside.

What could she do? Suddenly, she had an idea. Ellie veered into an alleyway off of the main street as the wave of spectators marched on. Why hadn't she thought of this before?

CHAPTER 8

9:45 a.m.

Detective Mark Ryan was not usually a worrier. Good or bad things would happen as they did. Worrying did nothing to affect the outcome. Though he wasn't much of a reader, he'd lived by a line he read while in high school from *To Kill a Mockingbird*. It was when Atticus Finch tells his young children, "It's not time to worry yet."

But it was time to worry, Ryan thought, as he sat at a workstation in an unmarked white van on Seventh Street, a block away from the jail. This was the mobile Unified Command Center which included Undersheriff Mitch Harrold, high ranking officers of the SRT or Special Reaction team, the SFFD chief, and Ryan and his partner, Perry, and other high-ranking law enforcement officials. ATF agents were on route to check out the bomb threats at the jail exits. And Jack Flynn, an FBI agent with the Joint Terrorism Task Force, was on his way.

Ryan rubbed his chin and found a small a bristly patch

he'd missed with his razor this morning. He then picked up his phone, checking for the hundredth time, hoping to see a text from Charlotte.

There weren't any.

Outside the van, the largest emergency response team that Ryan had ever seen in his fifteen years on the force was ready and waiting. Armies of uniformed police and first responders, EMS, firetrucks, ambulances, plus a SWAT team, and units from the city's crisis emergency team surrounded the area of the jail. Snipers were stationed atop buildings, hidden from view. It looked like a city under siege, and it was.

The suicide bomber was still in the jail lobby encased in explosives. He'd also claimed to have planted bombs near the overpass that led from the jail to the Hall of Justice, and at the jail's loading dock.

The Hall of Justice also housed a jail, the old jail, where inmates lived in crowded cells and had none of the rehabilitation programs of the new jail. Ryan's office in the Central Precinct was on the floor below. And numerous courthouses filled the other floors. The Hall had been swiftly evacuated, though not the inmates in the old jail.

As Ryan sat in the overcrowded van, he thought of Charlotte. He pictured her intelligent green eyes and the way they lit up her face. He thought of her lips and the last time he'd kissed them. Then he remembered how she'd pulled away, refusing to go further. "I can't do what my ex did to me," Charlotte said, knowing Ryan was still in a relationship with Olivia.

That relationship had ended weeks ago. But Charlotte didn't know it. Olivia said they needed a break. Ryan didn't disagree.

But he didn't want to go running from one relationship

to another. Instead, he'd deliberately avoided Charlotte. He'd made it a point not to walk in the direction of the jail on his lunch break. And when she texted, he answered with curt, one-word answers.

Now he wondered if he'd ever see her again.

No, he shook his head to dislodge the thought. Charlotte was tough, tougher than she looked at five feet two. He'd seen her face down killers before. He'd seen her put herself at risk to save her students. She would get through this. She had to.

The radio in the van crackled. They were patched into the jail's radio system. A familiar voice came through the line: Deputy Mary Jane Cunningham.

If there was one ray of hope, it was that Cunningham was on duty in the lobby and not some younger and more hot-headed deputy.

"We're remaining in a lockdown situation." Cunningham's voice was loud and calm. "No evacuations at this time. I have a new demand. Call off the bomb squad at east exit. I repeat, call off the bomb unit immediately."

"Cunningham." It was Captain Park. "We'd like to work on a—"

The channel went dead.

How had the terrorist known the bomb squad had been called? Had he somehow tapped into the security cameras? Or did he have partners on the outside?

The operation seemed too sophisticated for one person, but so far, there was no indication others were involved.

And just what did the bomber want? Other than locking down the jail and going to D pod, which was never going to happen.

Hundreds of inmates lived on the fourth floor of the jail in four separate pods—two for the men and two for the women. Ryan hoped the captain would comply with this latest request to call off the bomb squad at the rear exit. What other choice was there?

"It's got to be personal with this bomber," Ryan said to his partner, Perry. The two detectives were sitting side by side at their laptops in the crowded van.

"Either he has a grudge against the jail or wants to kill someone in custody or both," Ryan said more to himself than anyone else.

Perry nodded. "Yeah, but what's the end game here? Does he really think they'll just take him upstairs to D Pod?"

Her red hair had more gray streaks these days, something Ryan noticed but didn't comment on. Since Perry's twins had been born nearly two years ago, she had aged at an accelerated rate. She was thinner, paler, and sported purple circles under her eyes, but she rarely talked about her domestic life, and Ryan didn't ask.

"You think he's doing this to make some kind of political point about the prison-industrial complex?" Perry asked.

Ryan ran his hand through his thick dark hair. He usually wore it short, a military buzz cut, but he'd let it go. He wasn't so sure he liked this more laid-back version of himself.

"I don't think so. We know he knows the jail. He knew there were no metal detectors in the lobby—unlike the Hall. And he knows about the pod system in general and D pod in particular."

Ryan glanced at Undersheriff Harrold, who was standing over a captain and a senior deputy pulling up information about the inmates in D pod. Doing background research on them would take hours—hours they didn't have.

And Ryan knew the Sheriff's Office had other worries.

What to tell the families of those incarcerated. They owed them some communication.

"Maybe he's got an issue with a deputy or multiple deputies, and they're the targets," Ryan said. "Or maybe someone he knew died in custody and he's seeking revenge."

Ryan told Harrold they'd check recent deaths in the jail, though despite the media coverage, there weren't that many.

Ryan remembered that just before Charlotte had started working at the jail, an inmate had been found unresponsive. The medical examiner had determined the man had an undiagnosed heart condition, yet the family was suing the department, citing lack of medical treatment.

Ryan paused.

When had he started dividing his life into the time before Charlotte started teaching at the jail and the time after? What did this say about him and his feelings for Charlotte?

He hadn't realized he'd been thinking of a before Charlotte. And now it was impossible to imagine an after. He hoped he wouldn't have to.

CHAPTER 9

9:50 a.m.

Sergeant Chisholm and Deputy Lopez somehow corralled my students back inside the classroom. I tried to get them to sit in their seats—no more sitting under the desk—but they

ignored my request and instead stood around Chisholm, peppering him with questions.

"What are we gonna do? Wait here till we get blown up?" Erika asked.

"We're sheltering in place while we de-escalate the situation." Chisholm's response sounded like a plan, but I had doubts about who was going to de-escalate and why they hadn't done it in the last hour.

"Can we at least get some food?" Erika asked.

"I'll see what I can do."

That seemed to quiet some of the women. Chisholm took Lopez aside. Then the junior deputy left the classroom, probably to scrounge for snacks.

Chisholm looked at me. "You good?"

"Of course." If he was asking if I had anything to fear from my students, the answer was no. I never had.

But the women were scared. I was too, though I couldn't show it.

And just what were we supposed to do now?

"How can you think about eating at a time like this?" Leticia snapped at Erika. "I want to call my daughter. It's my goddamn last right."

"Let's not talk about last rites," I said. I'd never seen Leticia snap before. She was usually so calm. I didn't know if she meant last rite or last right, but either way, I hoped this wasn't the last of anything.

Who would I call for my last phone call? My sister Helen probably and hoped she'd answer. More than anything, I'd want to hear my nephew George's happy baby sounds. I'd tell my sister I loved her, that I was sorry I'd let her down months ago when I left George with my friend Sergio and went off to save one of my students.

If I got two phone calls, I'd call Ryan and tell him... tell him what? That every day I regretted pulling away from his kiss? That I thought of him night and day? That my entire body tingled when I thought of him? That I was sorry we'd never get to explore what might have been between us?

"So, what we supposed to do?" Aliyah had suddenly turned up at my side. Her face was bleeding where she'd picked at her acne. Since she'd entered my classroom, Aliyah was never far from my side, but she had a way of suddenly appearing that made me jumpy.

Good question. I needed to think of something. The atmosphere was too tense.

I'd managed to get the women to sit on the floor in a

circle. This felt better than having them at their desks as if it were a regular school day. But once on the floor, I realized we were like sitting ducks, a cliché that took on new meaning.

"How about we play a game?" I said.

"You mean like cards? They're back in the pod," Erika said. "I'll just go get them." She jumped up as if she were going to walk out of the classroom.

A few women chuckled.

"No. Like a party type of game." I tried to think of something. Charades?

Erika sat back down on the other side of me.

"How about two truths and a lie?" Aliyah whispered. "We used to play that with my friends."

This game wouldn't be my first choice—jail rules prohibited me from asking or answering personal questions —but I couldn't think of anything better.

"Yeah. I like that one," Erika said.

"OK," I said. "Does everyone know how to play?"

Leticia shook her head no.

"What's wrong with you, girl?" Erika asked. "It's right there in the name. You say three things about yourself and we have to guess. Two truths and a lie, get it?"

"It's been a while for me too," I said, looking at Erika and feeling Leticia's anger start to rise. "So, thank you for explaining. OK, who wants to go first?"

Erika's hand shot up. "Alrighty then," she said. "This is my first time in jail." The women laughed.

"Too obvious," I said.

"I'm just teasing you," Erika said. "OK, lemme think."

I glanced around at the women. Most were engaged. Their faces turned towards Erika.

"I grew up in Reno," Erika said. "I got eight brothers and sisters. I got busted for intent to sell."

I was about to protest and ask the women not to talk about their crimes when Leticia said, "Those are two lies. Everyone knows you didn't get busted for intent to sell. Not this time. And you didn't grow up in Reno, neither."

"Oh yeah." Erika laughed, an infectious laugh that came from deep within her belly. "I forgot. Two truths. See, I ain't good at math."

The mood had definitely lightened.

Just then, Lopez stuck his head in the classroom. "I got some snacks." He wheeled in a cart full of chips and packaged cookies.

The women jumped up and swarmed the cart. This was a rookie move on the deputy's part. You don't bring a cart full of coveted commissary items and not expect a group of hungry women to storm it. Lopez was overwhelmed as the women started grabbing the snacks.

"Let's distribute these fairly." Only Aliyah stayed seated as I stood next to the car.

Then I looked at Lopez, dismissing him. "We'll handle this."

I counted the bags on the cart and the number of students. "There's enough for two each. Let's do this one at a time."

Every woman took the small generic brands of popcorn, potato chips, and processed cakes and cookies—until there were none left. I handed the last two bags to Aliyah, who hadn't moved. She was rail thin and seemed more interested in biting her nails than biting into food.

When I sat back down, Erika said, "Where's yours, Ms. P.?"

I hadn't figured myself in the equation. "I'm alright."

"No. That's not fair," Aliyah said.

Erika handed me an unopened package of cheese puffs. Then other women passed down their packages of snacks. Bags of snacks piled up before me.

My eyes started to water. The stress of the morning combined with the women's generosity was too much.

"That's really sweet of you," I said. "But I'll just take a cookie from someone and give you back the rest."

No one moved, so I redistributed the snacks. The women took them reluctantly.

If you've ever been in a jail, and most people have not, you'd understand just how coveted packaged snacks are. Most women don't have money on their books to buy from the commissary. Most make do with the same jail food day after day.

Erika held out a cookie to me. I took it and thanked her.

"OK. Who'd like to go next?"

Aliyah was in my line of sight. I caught her eye, and she shrugged and put down her potato-chip bag.

"I have two kids."

The women laughed. I was pretty sure that was a lie. Aliyah was barely out of her teens, and there was nothing maternal about her. Quite the opposite. She was in need of mothering.

"I went to Mission High School."

Erika shook her head, indicating she thought this wasn't true. I noticed Aliyah didn't say she graduated high school, only that she attended. And based on what I knew of her reading ability, this was probably true. Most of my students had rarely made it past middle school.

A few women shrugged, unsure of whether this was true

or not, but most were busily munching away as they waited for Aliyah to deliver her last statement.

"I know someone who wants to bomb the jail."

"What did you say?" I asked Aliyah.

She looked down at her hands with their bloody cuticles resting in her lap. "I know someone who wanted to bomb the jail."

CHAPTER 10

10:00 a.m.

Detective Mark Ryan's ear was hot from holding his cell phone so close to it. Thanks to Cunningham's risky communication, they had the first three numbers—or thought they did—of the bomber's six-digit SFNO number. There were only a thousand permutations of possible numerals to go.

They were looking for recent male inmates whose intake number started with four zero six, and that had narrowed it down to eight hundred, give or take a few. It could take weeks, not hours or minutes, to find the bomber's identity. And they didn't have that kind of time.

Ryan was frustrated with how slowly the process was going. The Sheriff's department had only two IT guys on it, but Ryan had said he and Perry would take any names of those who'd died in custody and work that angle.

There were more than he'd thought—fifteen in the past ten years over all three jails. Many were suicides. He and Perry were locating next of kin, as perhaps the bomber had a vendetta against the jail for a loved one who'd died while incarcerated. It was a long shot, but any shot was worth taking.

Ryan wasn't always successful in reaching the next of kin. When he did, he'd been cursed at and hung up on. One woman threatened to sue the sheriff's department over her daughter's death. He apologized for her loss, and he meant it. Another older man had told him his son had been dead to him long before his actual death.

"What are we missing?" Ryan turned to Perry, who'd been equally unsuccessful in her attempts to locate any next of kin who might help fill in the blanks of the bomber's identity.

They'd replayed the conversation from Cunningham. Ryan found some comfort in hearing Cunningham's steady voice.

The FBI had been called in. Ryan had worked with one of the agents before—Special Agent James Flynn, who was also calling in a hostage negotiator. But so far, the bomber was refusing to talk to Flynn or anyone.

Though Cunningham hadn't been trained as a hostage negotiator, Ryan would put his money on her any day for her ability to talk the bomber down.

Ryan looked at his watch. He wore an old-fashioned Timex, which his mother had given him years ago when he made detective.

He was shocked to see it was after ten a.m. How had time passed so quickly in one way and not at all in another? Meanwhile, he was living the same tense minute over and over again. His stomach churned with anxiety and burned coffee.

Ryan tried to push aside the question that kept repeating in his mind. Would he get to see Charlotte again?

What Ryan felt for Charlotte was real. But he didn't want to be in a rebound relationship.

Instead, he did something Olivia had told him he'd needed to do many times: work on himself. He'd started seeing a therapist for the first time in his life. He was three sessions in and hated it.

His father, if he were alive, would have made fun of Ryan for seeing a shrink and smacked him on the head. Playfully, but a little too hard. As a boy, Ryan had been routinely smacked around by his dad and his uncles in the name of making a man of him.

But if he told his mother about Charlotte and seeing a therapist, Ryan was sure she'd approve of both.

Yet Ryan had told no one, not even Perry, that he'd finally taken advantage of the department's EAP, employee assistance program, to see a therapist confidentially. He knew he had commitment issues. Olivia had told him this several times.

Ryan always kept himself slightly aloof from the women he dated. He wasn't even necessarily aware he was being distant, but he'd heard the same complaint from the few women he'd been involved with over the years. "I feel like I don't even know you," one woman had said. "And you don't want me to. I feel like you keep yourself behind bulletproof glass."

Cold. Distant. Preoccupied with work. Emotionally unavailable. Ryan had been accused of all of these things. He wanted to be better for Charlotte. She deserved better.

Sitting in a hot van, sweat beading on his forehead and upper lip, Ryan wondered if it was too late. He should have told Charlotte about his breakup with Olivia. He could even have told her he was seeing a therapist. Charlotte would have understood.

He looked at his watch. One more minute had passed. Why the hell weren't they making progress?

Ryan checked his phone again, then threw it down on the makeshift desk. Perry looked at him, arching an eyebrow. She didn't have to say anything. There an entire conversation in the look she gave him.

With every second that passed, Ryan felt like he was the one imprisoned. And he'd done it to himself.

CHAPTER 11

10:03 a.m.

"That's a lie!" several women said after Aliyah's pronouncement. Looking into Aliyah's dark brown eyes, I wasn't so sure. Then she looked down at her hands again.

The circle of women suddenly grew quiet. Aliyah shrank into her oversized orange jail uniform as if she were trying to disappear.

"What you mean?" Erika asked.

Aliyah moved closer to me.

"Do you know someone who wanted to bomb the jail?" I asked gently.

Aliyah nodded yes.

"Is he a friend of yours?" I asked.

"Uncle." Her voice was a whisper. I bent my head close to hear her.

"OK. Uncle. What's his name?"

Had I pushed her too far? If she knew the bomber, then

my questioning could lead Aliyah into a legal trap. Accessory to terrorism? There must be such a thing.

Aliyah didn't respond. Instead, she picked at her cuticles, then ripped a tiny piece away. Bright red blood bloomed next to the nail on her index finger. This time, I put my hands over hers and kept them there.

"What's your uncle's name, Aliyah?" I asked again.

She looked up at the security camera in the corners. I followed her gaze. I doubted the deputies in the control room were looking at us. They had other things to worry about.

"Maltese," she finally said.

"That's a nice name," Erika said. "That his real name? Or, you know, like the poem where Stevie wasn't her real name."

Good question. I nodded my thanks to Erika.

"Just Maltese. That's his first name. Sometimes I call him Uncle Malt, but he doesn't like that."

"And what did he tell you?" I could sense Aliyah wanting to pick at her cuticles, but I refused to move my hand.

Erika shifted next to me. Leticia looked at me. We'd all been sitting incredibly still—but I sensed the women's growing restlessness with the slow pace of Aliyah's interrogation.

Finally, Aliyah raised her thin shoulders and shrugged. "Dunno."

"You must have some reason to think it might be your uncle. Did he say something about it?"

Erika sighed loudly. She was losing patience and seconds away from cursing at Aliyah. I pressed my leg against Erika's, hoping she'd get the message to keep quiet.

"Did your Uncle Maltese say something to you?"

Aliyah shrugged again. Her non-response was maddening.

I looked at the clock. Every minute that went by could bring us all closer to death.

I took a deep breath and tried again. "Does your uncle know you're here?"

Aliyah looked down into her lap.

"Shit." Erika stood up. "Yes or no?"

"No." Aliyah's lower lip trembled. "He don't know I been arrested. He wouldn't like that."

"OK." I glared at Erika to get her to sit down. "You're doing really well, Aliyah. I know this is hard for you."

"Tell me more about what your uncle said."

To my immense relief, Erika sat back down.

"You're not going to get in trouble," Erika told her. "We got you."

Aliyah finally looked up. First at Erika, then at me.

I nodded encouragingly.

"He said he hated this jail. Hated everyone in it. Said he wanted to blow it up cause of what they did. He was gonna do it too. Says he had it planned."

"Do you know what they did means?"

Aliyah shook her head no.

"What else did your uncle say?" I asked her gently.

Aliyah shrugged. "My mom didn't want me hearing no more. Said Uncle Maltese was a bad influence. Told me to go out 'cause she wanted to talk to him in private."

"When was this?"

Aliyah was trembling next to me.

I squeezed Aliyah's hand tighter. "You're not going to get in trouble. Promise. It's really important you tell us."

"After he got out. Like June, I think ... Aliyah's voice trailed off.

"OK. Aliyah, listen to me. I need to let the deputies know what you told me. You're not going to get in trouble. This could be important information, so I'm going to go tell them. OK?"

Aliyah's dark brown eyes filled with tears.

Blood rushed to my head when I stood up too quickly. My heart thumped in my chest. I ran to the door and stepped into the hallway.

Only Deputy Lopez was standing there.

"Call Chisholm," I told the deputy. "One of my students thinks she knows who the bomber is."

CHAPTER 12

10:08 a.m.

The alleyway stank of urine. Two rough-looking men sat side-by-side on the ground near Ellie, empty beer cans and syringes next to them.

Ellie turned away and glanced down at her phone. She'd missed a call. She didn't recognize the number, but fortunately they'd left a voicemail.

We're calling to report that your son, Max Flanigan, was absent for third period. Please call our attendance office to report any excused absences.

Fuck's sake. She tried to call Max. It went to voicemail. She had a list of things she wanted to ask, but she didn't leave a message.

She'd deal with it later. She'd stepped into the alley to make a different call.

Ellie tapped on her list of contacts, praying she'd get an answer.

"Hullo." Jazmyn's voice was a whisper.

Ellie was so shocked Jazmyn picked up she stuttered for a moment. Then she introduced herself.

"I know who you are." Jazmyn cut her off. "Why you calling me?"

"Well. Honestly, I didn't expect you to pick up. I called because I wanted to know how Charlotte is—how you all are," Ellie added, feeling inarticulate.

"We're all just dandy here." Jazmyn's husky smoker's voice dripped with sarcasm. "I'm trapped in my office waiting for some motherfucker to blow us up."

"Is Charlotte with you?"

"She's upstairs in class."

"Why haven't you evacuated?"

"I don't know. All's I know is we're locked in our offices and there's a terrorist in the lobby and nobody is telling us shit."

"Well, there's lots of activity outside. From what I see out on the street, the jail is surrounded by law enforcement and first responders." Ellie tried to sound reassuring.

"Lot of good it's doing so far," Jazmyn said.

"Do they know who the bomber is or what he wants?"

"I don't know. Like I said, we're locked down here and no one's giving us any information. My guess is some guy who's not playing with a full deck who has a beef with the jail and thinks it's a good idea to kill lots of innocent people."

"Is that what everyone thinks?"

"I don't know about everyone. I'm the only one in the office. Well, except for Will here. It's his first day. And the guy's about to have a heart attack."

"What do you mean?"

"He's sweating, looks pale. The guy's not a spring chicken, and he said something about his heart."

"Have you told Tony?"

"I know fuck-all about where Tony is," Jazmyn said. "Think the supervisor keeps me updated about his schedule? It's me and Will, and Belinda and the new admin and the only thing separating us from that maniac in the lobby is a cement wall. What do you think our chances are?"

"I don't know," Ellie admitted.

"That's what I thought." Jazmyn sounded resigned.

"Have you been in touch with the Sheriff or the Chief?"

"Yeah, they invited me to lunch."

"I mean, you have a cell phone. Have you talked to anyone?"

"Yeah. Talked to the Chief. Lot of good that did. Told us the lobby was sealed off, and that means we're sealed off. Supposedly they're bringing in a hostage negotiator. Like I said, we're stuck here and no one gives a good goddamn about us."

"I'm so sorry." Ellie wasn't sure what else to say. Then she asked, "Is there anything I can do?"

Jazmyn snorted. "Support my wife and kids after I'm gone?"

Charlotte had told Ellie about Jazmyn's four adopted children—all of whom were under the age of eight, who were birthed by the same drug-addicted mother who was now in prison.

"I wouldn't give up hope yet." Ellie said. Then she asked, "Who's on duty in the lobby?"

"Cunningham."

Ellie nodded. Charlotte had talked about the deputy. Like Jazmyn, Cunningham was a friend.

"Now, you got anything you can tell me?" Jazmyn asked.

"I spoke to Detective Ryan. There's a full response with

emergency vehicles, SWAT team, FBI, I think. I'll call you if I hear anything."

"You mean when you hear the bomb go off?" Jazmyn gave a short laugh. "Sure."

"Thanks, Jazmyn. I'm really sorry."

The line went dead. Ellie's goodbye sounded lame even to her ears. But what could she say?

One of the men on the sidewalk approached Ellie. "You got a cigarette?"

She shook her head no. The man didn't move.

Ellie wasn't afraid. She'd interviewed many unhoused men and women, even kids barely as old as her own boys.

Ellie looked down at the pavement and began to move around him.

"You got some bad news?" the man asked her gently.

Ellie looked up and met the man's gaze.

Her eyes grew moist with unshed tears. There was something unexpected about the man's question and the gentle way he asked that moved her.

San Francisco was a city of contrasts and contradictions. Stunning beauty. Squalor and homeless encampments. Obscene wealth for some. Poverty for others.

Ellie felt a rush of warmth towards the man. She didn't have a cigarette, and she never gave money, but she reached in her purse, found a tin of mints, and handed it to him.

"Thank you," he said sincerely.

Ellie walked back out of the alley. As she fought the tide of pedestrians heading away from the jail, Ellie's phone buzzed. She didn't recognize the number.

Is Charlotte OK? This is Sergio. Is she safe?

Sergio, Charlotte's mechanic and friend, the one who'd helped save her life. Charlotte had brought him to a July

Fourth BBQ they'd hosted, and he texted the next day to thank her, which she thought was polite.

Ellie's thumbs hovered above her phone. What could she type in response? *No,* was the simple answer. But that message was best delivered in a phone call.

CHAPTER 13

10:10 a.m.

"She thinks she knows the bomber?" Sergeant Chisholm asked me for the second time.

I nodded.

"What's her name?"

"Aliyah."

Chisholm stepped around me quickly and stuck his head in the classroom. He called Aliyah, mispronouncing her name, so it came out like Eh-ya, rather than A-lee-ah, with three syllables.

It was several long moments before Aliyah stood up. And several more after that before she walked towards the door.

This was a mistake. I should have been the one to call her into the hallway.

Aliyah was moving so slowly, clutching her stomach, and curling in on herself as if she were going to be sick.

We didn't have this kind of time.

Luckily, Erika stood up too and put her arm around

Aliyah and walked her through the small classroom into the hallway. Deputy Lopez closed the door behind them.

I put my arm around Aliyah, who was shaking so much I needed to steady her.

"What do you know about the bomber?" Chisholm asked. I was expecting him to shout, but he'd lowered his voice, bending towards Aliyah, who shrank into herself even more.

"Nothing." Her voice was a whisper. "Nothing for sure," Aliyah added.

I opened my mouth in disbelief, then looked at Aliyah. "You told us you thought the man in the lobby might be your uncle, right?"

Aliyah shrugged her thin shoulders. She looked down at the polished floor as if seeking the answers there.

"You did," Erika said. "You said his name was Maltese."

Aliyah nodded.

Chisholm asked, "And why do you think your uncle Maltese might be the person in the lobby?" I appreciated that he didn't use the words bomber or terrorist.

Maddeningly, Aliyah shrugged again.

Was she lying about her uncle to get attention? I doubted it. Aliyah was never one to draw attention to herself. If anything, she tried to make herself disappear, to chip away at her body.

"Why don't you tell Sergeant Chisholm what you told me, Aliyah?" I asked. "Can you do that?"

This time she nodded.

"He been in jail. This jail. Like me. But he got out and he told my mom that he had a plan. He hated everyone. He wanted to blow it up cause..."

We waited for Aliyah to continue her sentence. But she didn't.

"Your uncle Maltese said he wanted to bomb the jail?" Chisholm asked.

Aliyah nodded.

"Did he say why?" Chisholm asked.

"Not really. Not to me. Just that he hates the place. That's what he said. He gonna get even for what they did."

"When did he say this?" Chisholm asked.

"Like a couple of months ago. When he got out."

"Is Maltese your mom's brother?" Chisholm asked.

"Yeah. I don't see him much no more. We're not like a close family..." Aliyah looked down at her hands. If I hadn't been holding one, she would have started picking at her fingers.

"Your uncle doesn't know you're here in jail, right now?" I asked.

"No. He wouldn't like it." Aliyah finally looked up. She kept her eyes on my face.

"Because of what happened to him here?" I wanted to see if there was anything else Aliyah could tell us.

"I don't know what happened to him. I know my mom was crying a lot. About him. About me too. She kept saying, 'why do I hang out with bad people, stay out all night? I could end up in jail like Maltese.'"

"Do you know anyone who could be helping your uncle?" Chisholm asked.

Aliyah shrugged again. "Probably. He knows some very bad people."

"People who might be helping him get revenge?" Chisholm asked.

"Maybe," Aliyah said. "I don't know."

"Do you know who these people are?" Chisholm asked.

Aliyah shook her head no. "I don't know anything else. I told you."

"One more thing," Chisholm asked. "What's your uncle's full name?"

"Maltese Anthony Jones."

The sergeant then asked Aliyah what her uncle looked like, where he lived, and any other information she could give him.

Aliyah filled in the blanks about her uncle's physical description but didn't know his address or where he last worked. But she gave her mother's name, address, and phone number.

Chisholm looked at me and nodded.

"You've been very helpful, Aliyah," the sergeant said. "You can go back into the classroom now."

I told Erika and Aliyah I'd join them in a minute and waited until the classroom door was closed.

Chisholm had already grabbed his walkie-talkie.

"What happens now?" I asked.

He held out his hand for me to be quiet as he relayed the information he'd learned about Aliyah's mother and uncle.

"You think she's telling the truth?" Lopez asked.

"I don't think she'd lie."

"Thanks," Chisholm had finished his call and turned to leave. Then he stopped and looked at me. "Hey," he said, "if it is Maltese, we'll have you to thank for that information."

And if it wasn't, then where did that leave us?

CHAPTER 14

Sixty minutes since lockdown

Cunningham needed to sit down. It had been over an hour since the bomber had entered the lobby and shown his vest full of explosives, nearly an hour since the jail had been locked down, and forty-five minutes since she'd been actively stalling about complying with the guy's demands to go upstairs to D pod.

"You understand when we're on lockdown, the elevators are out, right?" Cunningham told the bomber. "And the automatic doors are locked. They're trying to override the system to make them function again so we can get you upstairs."

That was Cunningham's first lie. She told other untruths about Sheriff Nicky O'Connor wanting to talk to him and who would call soon to see to his demands.

Cunningham did everything but tap dance for the bomber trying to distract him. And part of it was working. He didn't seem quite so jumpy, quite so electric since he'd been waiting. Nor did he strike her as all that forceful.

She'd talked him into letting the civilians in the offices stay locked away, assuring him that any damage he'd do in the lobby would be equally destructive to the offices and the people in them. That seemed to mollify him.

But there could be no more stalling. Cunningham sensed the bomber's growing impatience. And she didn't feel like getting blown up today. She'd have to think of something else.

She was about to suggest they both sit down when the radio crackled and her captain's voice came through.

"Cunningham, we have some new information we'd like to share with the man in the lobby. Can you put him on?"

The bomber shook his head no.

"You talk," he told Cunningham.

"He's listening." Cunningham kept her finger on the talk button. "What is it captain?"

"We have a young woman in custody. Aliyah Sonera. She's upstairs. Says she's your niece."

The bomber shook his head no.

Shit, Cunningham thought. Was this wild guess the sheriff's department's best guess? The bomber shook his head again and took a step back.

"No," he said. "I don't believe you."

"Maltese," the Captain said.

The bomber startled at his name. Bullseye, Cunningham thought.

"Maltese. Your niece is upstairs. You wouldn't do anything to hurt her, would you?"

"I want to talk to her," the bomber said. "Now."

∾

RYAN WAS PACING in the cramped mobile command center van when the information came through. They had a name: Maltese Anthony Jones. And surveillance footage from the lobby—before the bomber had blacked out the cameras—showed the bomber fit the general description they'd been given of his height and build.

"How'd we get the name.?" Ryan asked the team.

FBI Agent Jack Flynn was the first to answer.

"Friend of yours, teacher named Charlotte Papadapa something..." Flynn said.

"Papadopoulous." Ryan cut him off. He didn't know Flynn well, and he didn't like the man's cavalier way of cutting short Charlotte's long Greek surname. He was also surprised that Flynn knew he had any relationship with Charlotte. Who leaked this information, he wondered? And just how did Flynn know?

"What does Charlotte have to do with this?" Ryan asked.

"Bomber's related to one of her students. Apparently, the niece said her uncle had been in jail. Got released. Had some grudge and that's probably why he wants to blow up D pod," Flynn said. "He wants niece to go downstairs to the lobby."

"Then what?"

"We'll prep her before she talks to him. Meanwhile we've got to get this guy Maltese's sister and anyone else we can find."

"And Charlotte?" Ryan asked.

Flynn was silent for a moment. "She did good. We have her to thank."

Ryan nodded.

"See what else you can find on this Anthony guy," Flynn said.

PERRY'S FINGERS flew over the keys on her laptop as she searched the NCIC, the national crime information center database, pulling up everything she could find on Maltese Anthony Jones, the suspected bomber.

Ryan paced impatiently behind her.

"Arrested February 2024 for petty theft. Charged with misdemeanor. Served almost four months. Had a couple of drug infractions two years before that. Always cited out and didn't serve time."

Perry's fingers hovered over the keyboard. "And here's something else—this Maltese guy was questioned in relation to a gang bombing in the Mission. Never arrested. But interviewed as a person of interest."

"I don't remember a bombing in the Mission," Ryan said. "When was this?"

"2020. We should ask Flynn what he knows. The feds arrested two Norteños gang members. Found explosive materials but no bombs. Apparently, they were planning on going DEFCON on another gang but hadn't yet pulled it off."

Ryan nodded. He vaguely recalled the case. It wasn't his, and Maltese wouldn't have crossed his desk in homicide. In fact, the guy had been able to remain just under the radar, skirting the line between felonies and misdemeanors, associating with gang members, but not getting caught. And the bomb information was relevant.

"Any fights while in custody?" Ryan asked.

"Nothing," Perry said. "That's what's odd. If something happened in jail, it would be in his record. Instead, he was released early on good behavior."

So what was Maltese's motive? Was it gang-related?

The pieces of the puzzle were snapping together. But not completely. They didn't have all the pieces yet.

Even with the stakes this high, Ryan loved this part of an investigation, when his brain was firing on all cylinders, when puzzled pieces started to fit to create a full picture.

Adrenaline coursed through his veins, making him feel alive. All of his senses were on high alert.

Just then, Ryan's phone buzzed. It took him a moment to recognize the number—Helen, Charlotte's sister. He stabbed at the phone. Maybe she'd heard from Charlotte.

"Detective Ryan?" Helen's voice sounded a lot like Charlotte's. And for a moment, Ryan's heart skipped a beat.

Then he heard a kid's TV show in the background.

"It's Helen, Charlotte's sister. We met at the hospital when Charlotte was..." Helen's voice trailed off.

"I remember. How can I help?"

"I'm so worried. I tried to call Charlotte and she's not picking up. I heard on the news about the bomber. Is Charlotte safe?"

Ryan shook his head, though Helen couldn't see it. "I can tell you we're working on a solution. We've got all the resources—"

"So, Charlotte is at the jail? I knew it wasn't safe for her to work there. How did this happen?"

"Helen. We're doing our best to get everyone out safely, including Charlotte. Can you do something for me?" While Ryan needed nothing from Helen, he'd found that giving someone a job in a crisis helped calm them down.

"Will you turn off the news and keep your phone close by in case Charlotte contacts you?"

Helen didn't respond.

"Try not to worry," he said. "I know it's hard. I need you to stay calm. For Charlotte," Ryan added.

"Will you call me when you hear anything?"

"I promise. You take care of yourself and George."

Ryan hung up.

While he'd been talking to Helen, the rest of the mobile command team was gathered over a computer.

"What's going on?" Ryan asked.

"Maltese Anthony's jail number didn't start with four zero six," Perry told him.

"So the man in the lobby isn't Anthony?"

"We don't know," Undersheriff Harrold said.

CHAPTER 15

10:15 a.m.

Ellie was just about to call Sergio when her phone vibrated in her hand.

"Have you heard from Charlotte?" Sergio didn't say hello, but Ellie recognized his voice. She'd met Charlotte's mechanic friend only once, but she felt as if she knew him from all of Charlotte's stories about him.

Sergio had been away for several months, visiting his family in Bulgaria, and Ellie had sometimes felt she'd been Sergio's replacement, though that wasn't entirely fair.

"Sergio?"

"Yeah. I heard about the jail. Charlotte. Is she OK?" Sergio spoke with an Eastern European accent that seemed stronger than she remembered.

"We don't know," Ellie said truthfully. "I don't think they've evacuated, but first responders are everywhere, a SWAT team, and—"

"I come down."

"You won't be able to get near the jail."

"Where are you?"

"I'm at..." Ellie looked around. She was on Harrison Street between Ninth and Tenth, near the alleyway she'd ducked into. She squinted to read the sign for the alley. It had been graffitied over.

"I'm on Harrison and Ninth."

"I come to you."

"No—"

Sergio had already hung up.

Ellie sighed. She understood Sergio's need to be close, but there was nothing he could do, nothing she could do either.

Just as she went to put her phone in her purse, it rang again.

"What'ya got for me?" Bates McGuire also didn't bother with hellos.

"Not much," Ellie had to admit.

"Well, write something. Anything. You've got contacts. Use them." Bates hung up without a goodbye either. Like her son Jake, she thought. Unappreciative.

Ellie stood paralyzed on Harrison Street. In one direction was her office at the Herald, where Bates clearly wanted her. In the other was the jail, where her heart told her she needed to be.

Ellie didn't have a story yet. It wasn't that Ellie had writer's block, something she didn't believe in. Writing was a job like anything else. It was impossible to shape what was happening because it was personal and raw. And it wasn't over.

An image of Max flashed in her mind. She felt guilty that she'd momentarily forgotten about his anxiety and struggles.

She tried to find him on her phone app, but he'd

stopped sharing his location. When had he done that? Today? Yesterday? She couldn't remember the last time she'd tried to find him. He'd been home in his room for most of the summer. No mystery there.

What had she done wrong as a mother? How had she failed Max?

Stop that, she told herself. It wouldn't help to blame herself.

Ellie exhaled and said, "Fuck it."

Bates and his deadline would have to wait. Max would have to wait. There was nothing she could do about either now.

As she stood on the corner waiting for Sergio, Ellie realized it had gotten very warm. She suddenly felt as if she were being microwaved from within. *Fuck's sake!* She'd been getting hot flashes for about a month now. She tried not to believe they had anything to do with her upcoming forty-fifth birthday and changing hormones.

She ripped off her jacket, feeling as if she would combust right there on the sidewalk if she didn't get her clothes off. She heard a distinctive ripping sound as she did so, as the lining sheared away from the inside of the jacket.

Ellie felt like throwing her jacket on the ground and stomping on it. She'd had enough stress this morning. Max. Charlotte and the maniac bomber wanting to blow up the jail. The man whose Honda she supposed hit who'd probably sue her. And Bates breathing down her neck to file a story. It was all too much.

Ellie brushed away the hot tears that clouded her vision. They kept coming.

She fished around in her purse for a tissue, and not finding one, angrily dumped the contents on the sidewalk.

The next thing she knew, there was someone next to her, scooping up lipstick, eyes,

heartburn tablets, pens, other detritus from her purse. Sergio.

Sergio handed her a fresh tissue.

Ellie sat down on the curb. Sergio joined her.

She could see why Charlotte liked him. He was a big bear of a man with bushy eyebrows in need of a trim and thick black and white hair that fell around his face.

"Better?" he asked after she'd blown her nose.

Ellie nodded. Then she rested her head on Sergio's shoulder and closed her eyes. Just for a minute.

It felt so good to lean on someone, Ellie realized. When had she last allowed herself to do that? She tried so hard to hold it all together for her family. She was the sole bread-winner. And head cheerleader for her husband's flagging job search. Chief worrier about her boys, particularly Max.

Ellie knew she was strong. She also recognized the same strength in Charlotte, the same gritting your teeth and pushing through no matter what life dealt you.

But how nice to have an actual shoulder to lean on. Ellie thought about sharing this insight with Charlotte and prayed she'd get the chance.

CHAPTER 16

10:18 a.m.

We stood in the hallway waiting for Chisholm to get off the radio. He'd walked down the hallway, out of earshot. I was still holding Aliyah's hand in mine. It was cold.

Next to us, the women had pressed their faces against the glass wall at the back of the classroom. They weren't shy about eavesdropping.

"We've confirmed Maltese was held in D pod and released May 29th. That sound about right"

Aliyah nodded. Then shrugged. Her gestures were maddening, but I took it as a yes. As did Chisholm.

"So, we think it's your uncle in the lobby, and we'd like you to talk to him on the radio. See if we can't straighten this out before anyone gets hurt. Alright?"

Aliyah looked at me, then at Chisholm.

I nodded at her encouragingly. "You can do this."

"You're going to stay with me?" Aliyah asked, gripping my hand tighter.

"Yes. I'll be right here. I'm not going anywhere."

"Here's what's going to happen," Chisholm said. "We're going to have you talk to Agent Flynn first. He's with the FBI, and he's going to prep you on what to say to your uncle. Then we're going to radio to your uncle downstairs and say you want to talk to him."

Aliyah caught her breath in a strangled sob and shook her head no.

"All you have to do is talk to him. You can do it." I squeezed her hand tighter, trying to convey I believed she was up for this life or death mission. I had my doubts.

Chisholm waited a minute, then he spoke to someone on the radio and handed it to Aliyah.

"Aliyah, this is FBI Agent James Flynn." An authoritative voice echoed in the hallway.

Aliyah held the radio away from her ear as if it might bite.

"When you to talk to your uncle. Here's what I'd like you to say." Flynn's tone was direct, assertive.

We listened as Flynn spelled it out. Aliyah was to keep her uncle talking. She was to talk about the people in the jail, the other women, her teacher, the deputies who had been nice to her. Her job was to humanize the people in the jail—the very people her uncle wanted to kill.

Then Aliyah should talk about her mother—Maltese's sister—and their family. Remind her uncle of all the good times they've had, of the love they share, and most importantly that they don't kill people in their family—and that there was a way out of this.

Then came the third thing. Aliyah needed to persuade her uncle to stand down. He hadn't harmed anyone yet, including himself, and he needed to keep it that way. He could surrender peacefully.

"Remind him he has options," Flynn said. "We need to give him a way out."

Flynn asked Aliyah to repeat back what he said, and my heart sank. My student's voice was shaky and barely audible. I had to strain to hear it and I was only inches away.

She also repeated only about a quarter of the information Flynn told her to convey to her uncle.

My heart and spirits sank. This was never going to work. And how many of our previous five minutes had been spent on this?

"Remember the most important part?" I couldn't help myself and jumped in.

My student shook her head no.

"The most important part is to be yourself when you talk. Tell your uncle this isn't what your family wants, this isn't who you are, and it's not the way to solve problems. You want to remember that he doesn't have to kill innocent people."

Aliyah nodded.

"Ready over there?" Flynn's growing irritation was clear.

Aliyah nodded.

Chisholm would talk to Cunningham, then hand the radio to Aliyah.

"Cunningham. Chisholm here. We have someone upstairs who'd like to talk to Maltese who's in the lobby with you. His niece, Aliyah Sonera, who's in A Pod."

The deputy didn't respond immediately.

"Uh. Roger that."

My spirits rose when I heard the welcome sound of Cunningham's voice.

Then the radio went silent.

Had something gone horribly wrong? Maybe it wasn't Aliyah's uncle in the lobby?

Finally, the radio crackled to life, and Cunningham spoke. "No can do," she said. "Mr. Maltese wants Aliyah to come down to the lobby. He'll give you five minutes."

The radio went dead.

CHAPTER 17

10:20 a.m.

hisholm didn't look as shocked as I was. I'd just assumed that if the bomber were Maltese, he'd want to talk to his niece. The Sargeant looked as if he'd expected this outcome. He shook his head and strode off down the hallway, no doubt to speak to Flynn in private.

Lopez had gone into the classroom to get the women away from the glass wall and back in their seats.

I stood in the hallway too stunned to say anything. What was there to say? Aliyah curled her body closer to me as if seeking shelter.

Time was ticking. Five minutes. Four.

Chisholm stepped down the hallway to speak to Flynn just out of earshot. The three of us stood there.

"If it's not Maltese, then who?" I heard Chisholm say. And then something about a jail number.

"Flynn wants to speak to you again." Chisholm returned, holding out the radio. Aliyah didn't immediately take it, and

I had to stop myself from wresting it from the sergeant and shoving it at my student.

"Aliyah?" Flynn said.

"Yeah," her voice was soft.

"There's been a slight change of plan. We're still going to have you say all those things I told you about, remember?"

Aliyah nodded yes.

"Good, but now you're going to go down to the lobby and tell your uncle in person. You think you can do that?" Flynn asked.

Aliyah shook her head. "No."

Three minutes.

"No. I don't want to go alone."

"I'll go with her," I said. What choice did we have?

"You don't have to ..." Chisholm said.

"I'll go with Miss P." Aliyah said.

It was then I wondered, was this some kind of intricate escape plan she'd hatched with her uncle? And had I just fallen into a trap?

I didn't have time to think about this. Every second brought us closer to our deadline.

As I stood in the hallway, I turned and looked at the classroom with my students in their bright orange uniforms. And I thought of the original meaning of the term. *Deadline.* It was used during the Civil War to refer to an actual line, a boundary in prison beyond which soldiers would be shot if they crossed it.

Was I crossing my own deadline? Would I be blown up? Or would I see my students again?

"Put your teacher on." Flynn's voice cut through my thoughts.

Aliyah handed me the radio.

"You OK with taking Aliyah to the lobby?" I appreciated Flynn's question—and giving me an out if I wanted it.

Flynn quickly gave me instructions on what I was to say and do. Basically, say nothing. Do nothing. No fast moves. No moves at all.

"Got that?"

"Yes." It wasn't hard to remember.

"OK. Good. There's someone here who wants to talk to you," Flynn said.

"Charlotte?" I turned my back on the others in the hallway as soon as Ryan said my name.

"Ryan?" My voice broke.

"You sure you want to do this?"

"Do I have a choice?"

"You do," he said, but we both knew that wasn't true.

"We've got to a get move on," Flynn interrupted.

"Take care of yourself, and I'll see you when this is over, alright?" Ryan asked.

"Alright," I said, though neither of us sounded very sure.

"And Charlotte, we're not sure ..." the line went dead.

What was Ryan about to say? What wasn't he sure about?

Hearing him say my name so tenderly, I suddenly felt I was making a huge mistake. Wasn't it safer for me to stay on the fourth floor? If Maltese detonated the bomb, wouldn't I have better odds separated by layers of concrete than face-to-face in the lobby?

Ryan had been curt in our recent text exchanges, but there was none of that coldness in his voice. Would I ever get the chance to tell him how I felt?

"We've got to move." Chisholm's command cut through my thoughts.

I took one last look at my students through the glass.

They were all watching me. With more courage than I felt, I waved and smiled.

Then I grabbed Aliya's hand and followed Chisholm down the hall.

He stopped by a door near the elevator that I'd never noticed before.

"Elevators are stopped during lockdown," he explained. "You'll have to take the stairs."

Then he put his hand on my shoulder and asked Aliyah to wait a moment as he pulled me aside.

"Be very careful. We aren't 100 percent sure this guy is Maltese. He ticks a lot of the boxes, but you need to know. You want out? You tell me now."

The blood rushed to my head as my heartbeat roared in my ears. Then I looked over at Aliyah. She seemed sure it was her uncle, and I believed her. I felt it in my gut. But it wouldn't be the first time I'd misplaced my trust in a student.

"No," I said. "I don't want out."

"OK." Chisholm and I walked back to where Aliyah stood waiting.

Then the sergeant unlocked the door and held it open.

"Good luck," he said.

Aliyah entered the stairwell, and I followed closely behind.

CHAPTER 18

10:22 a.m.

"She has to know she could be walking into a trap," Ryan shouted at Flynn. The two men were standing outside the mobile command center van, the sliding door open for air.

"She's a civilian," Ryan continued. "She's not trained. And for all we know this is some scam and the niece is in on it."

"I don't think so." Flynn shook his head.

"And what tells you that?" Ryan snapped.

"Instinct," Flynn said. "You had no right to try to sow doubts and tell her. Look we don't know what number Anthony was spouting in the lobby. Could be a jail number. Not his. We're working on it. But we do know he served time, fits the description, and the niece thinks it's him."

Ryan exhaled and glanced down Seventh Street towards the jail, wishing he could see inside the lobby. Then he ran his hand through his hair

A million things could go wrong with this plan. Flynn

didn't know Charlotte, as he did. She was not one to follow orders. Or keep her mouth shut. And even if he had warned her, he knew she wouldn't change her mind anyway.

Ryan exhaled loudly.

"Let's get back to work," Flynn said, stepping inside the van.

Ryan lingered outside in the bright sunlight. His stomach clenched in fear and worry.

ELLIE PICKED up speed as she headed towards the jail. Sergio, by her side, matched her pace. Yes, she was literally running towards danger instead of away from it. And she should have been at her desk, as Bates insisted. But Ellie needed to be near Charlotte—or as close as was safely possible.

As she jogged, Ellie held her hand on her abdomen, where a stitch in her side pierced her. She slowed down her pace to a fast walk, but the cramp didn't go away.

Ellie's phone buzzed in her bag. She fished it out.

"Max," Ellie said, answering immediately as she saw his name on the screen. "What's up? Are you home? Where are you?"

"What are you doing?" he asked.

"I'm ... uh walking fast. I thought you were going home."

"Not yet. We were just hanging out at the school. I was talking to Nate and we figured out that they messed up my schedule, Mom. They put me in all the wrong classes, not even honors classes, and—"

"That's great," Ellie cut him off. "I'm so glad you worked it all out."

"No. I didn't work it all out." Max sounded annoyed. "Not yet.

"Do you need my help or dad's?" Ellie asked.

"I don't need your help or Dad's," Max snapped back. "I was just trying to tell you."

"No. Of course you don't need our help." Why was Ellie always jumping in? Always trying to solve her kids' problems for them?

"I'm calling cause you texted me like a thousand times," Max said.

"Not a thousand. Only several hundred."

Max laughed. So, she hadn't completely alienated him.

"I'm gonna go back inside and ask the counselor to fix it or something."

"I'm proud of you." Ellie's eyes grew moist. "But I really do have to go, sweetheart. I'll see you tonight."

Ellie exhaled with relief as she dropped her phone into her bag. At least one worry of the day had been solved. When would she learn that Max wasn't a child any longer? Maybe Ben was right. She smiled, thinking of telling him that.

Now if only everything else today would work out.

Feeling lighter than she did a moment ago, Ellie grabbed Sergio's arm and hurried towards the police blockade.

I'D NEVER TRANSPORTED one of my students anywhere in the jail before. I wasn't allowed to. Only movement deputies could move inmates from one area to the next.

So, it felt surreal to be walking down the stairs with Aliyah. Her bright orange flip-flops, the only shoes inmates were allowed to wear, slapped on the metal stairs as we descended. I grabbed her tighter so she wouldn't trip.

My heart beat too fast. I felt sick to my stomach. And I wasn't entirely sure I wasn't being played. Was this some elaborate plan to break Aliyah out of jail?

I looked at her in her bright orange sweats and quickly dismissed the idea. Jail wasn't prison. Aliyah was probably in on drug charges and couldn't make bail. She'd serve a few months at most.

No that wasn't the reason Maltese wanted to bomb the jail. He must have other reasons for wanting to kill us all.

Aliyah's hand was clammy in mine. Her thin fingers were like ice. A sheen of sweat shone across her face, full of acne and scabs where she'd picked at her skin.

As we walked down the four long flights of stairs, I tried not to imagine this might be the last day I'd ever see my students. I'd grown so fond of the women and found my calling when I started working at the jail less than a year ago.

My passion for teaching the women at the jail was the main reason I'd turned down a chance to be an assistant professor, something my dissertation advisor didn't understand. Nor advise. Nor did my sister, who asked me when I was going to get a real job at a university.

Only Ryan understood my need to be at the jail. He'd asked me about my dissertation and on our first date, which wasn't really a date at all but a spontaneous lunch. He seemed to get it. And to understand me in a way my ex never did.

Would I get the chance to tell Ryan how I really felt about him? How I longed to be with him? How I regretted pulling away when we kissed?

Stop it, I told myself. *Now's not the time.*

I hadn't realized I'd shaken my head until Aliyah turned and looked at me.

"You alright, Ms. P.?"

"Yeah," I said. "You?"

Aliyah shrugged in a way that could have meant anything.

When we were descending the last few stairs, Aliyah suddenly jerked my hand and pulled me down.

She was losing her balance. Her flip-flops slid on the slippery steps.

I managed to hold on to her and right her before both tumbled down.

"Sorry, Miss P.," she said. "I couldn't help it." She pointed to her flip-flops.

"Can you take those off?" I said.

She kicked them off, and we left them there on the stairs. Her socks weren't much better, but socks and flip-flops were a lethal combination.

We were now on the first floor in a small antechamber off the stairway and elevators. Only two short hallways and two heavy, reinforced metal doors separated us from a suicide bomber in the lobby.

Was Cunningham alright? Jazmyn? Will, the new teacher?

I would know soon enough and see just what madness I'd volunteered for.

Out of habit, I held up my jail clearance to the surveillance camera in the corner. I wore the laminated badge on a chain around my neck. It occurred to me that this might be the last time I ever did so.

I probably needed have bothered. The deputies were following our every move on surveillance cameras.

The lock on the first heavy steel door snapped open. We

passed through and into a small hallway. Then the second door released with a loud buzz. Aliyah startled and grabbed onto me.

"It's OK," I said, releasing her death grip on my arm.

A few steps later, we passed by an empty control room. This is where deputies sat behind bulletproof glass and controlled entry through the doors.

Today, the small control room was empty. It made sense. They were close to the lobby. In twenty feet, we'd be face to face with the bomber.

Aliyah stopped suddenly. Was she having second thoughts? We couldn't turn back now.

We could be killed in the lobby or killed here if Maltese detonated the bomb. I'd rather be killed in the lobby, I thought.

"OK. Let's take a deep breath," I said.

I took Aliyah's other hand and faced her.

"Like this." I inhaled slowly, held it for a few seconds, then exhaled slowly. Did we have time for this? No, but I wasn't sure what else to do.

I took an exaggerated breath again. And another one. We were running out of time. I hoped these deep breaths wouldn't be my last.

Finally, on the next inhale, Aliyah joined me.

After a few more breaths, I felt my student relax. Her breathing slowed. Her shoulders dropped several inches.

"Ready?"

Aliyah nodded.

Then I turned, and still holding my student's hand, walked towards the lobby.

CHAPTER 19

10:30 a.m.

It's a strange thing to think you may be walking towards your imminent death. My life didn't flash before my eyes, but I did suddenly think of my parents. Mine wasn't an altogether happy childhood. I escaped into books, but I loved my parents and realized I hadn't called them in a while.

Then I thought of my sister, Helen, and nephew, George. Would I see any of my family again?

Every person in the jail was probably thinking similar thoughts, I realized. Would they make it out of the jail alive? Would they get to hold their loved ones again?

I shook my head to dislodge these thoughts.

Yet the answers to these questions all depended on what Aliyah and I did next.

We were no more than fifteen feet from the lobby. When we turned the corner, we would be face-to-face with a suicide bomber.

IT HAD BEEN ten long minutes since Ryan had said goodbye to Charlotte. He paced outside the mobile command center, desperate to know what was happening inside the jail. But still waited until he could calm himself down.

Despite all the rescue vehicles, fire trucks, squad cars, EMTs, as far as the eye could see, it was quiet, as if the very city was holding its breath.

Were Charlotte and Aliyah in the lobby? Was Charlotte trying to reason with the maniac? He wouldn't be surprised.

Ryan had never felt so useless. It was a word he hated, a word his father had flung at him, that landed harder than his father's fists. Ryan was not a violent man—he'd sworn never to strike a blow unless in self-defense—but right now he felt like punching something. Hard. Instead, he clenched and unclenched his fists as he trod the same circular path on the sidewalk next to the van.

Why hadn't they heard anything? It was maddening there was no surveillance in the jail lobby. The bomber had seen to that. And so far, no update from Sergeant Chisholm. Nothing from Cunningham. Every second was agony.

The voice of Ryan's ex-girlfriend, Olivia, suddenly popped into his head. "Why can't you ever relax? You're always so tense."

Ryan had difficulty being off the clock, and letting himself truly relax. It was not in his nature. His nature was vigilant, born from growing up in a home with unpredictable violence, drug use, and criminal activity.

And now what good was all his vigilance?

Why was he thinking about this now? He should save it for his new therapist, a word—and concept—he found difficult to fit into his vocabulary.

Just then, the radio came to life in the van. Ryan sprinted towards the command center door.

ALIYAH GASPED when we entered the lobby. I did too. I had no idea the bomber would be wearing a black balaclava, the kind that terrorists wore on TV. Nor did I fully envision the reality of the man before me—a nervous-looking man with a chest wired with explosives. My insides turned to jelly.

Aliyah halted as soon as she saw the bomber. Did she recognize her uncle behind the mask? If not, it was too late for us to turn around and go back upstairs. We had come this far and were now face to face with a killer.

Deputy Cunningham nodded at us.

"It's alright," she said in her calm voice.

"Uncle?" Aliyah whispered.

The bomber stood about eight feet away from us, positioned in the center of the lobby, probably to do the most damage.

"'Liyah?" I'd never heard anyone call my student by a nickname. "What are you doing here?"

We'd been told not to move suddenly, not to approach the bomber, but Aliyah took a step closer to her uncle. Since I was still holding my student's hand, I did as well.

Not that I wanted to be any closer to the bomber. My eyes zeroed in on the small iPhone-like device Maltese held in his hand. His thumb was poised above the home button.

One tiny press and none of us would survive.

"I'm sorry, Uncle." Aliyah whispered. "I messed up."

"It's alright baby," he said. Maltese's voice was surprisingly tender. If this were an act, they were both Academy Award winners. "You're young."

Then Maltese jerked his chin at me.

"This is Miss P., my teacher," Aliyah said louder. "I like her. She's a good teacher, Uncle."

"You're new. You're in A pod, right?" Cunningham asked Aliyah. I held my breath to see if Maltese would react to the deputy's question. But he didn't.

"Yeah. I been in only thirteen days," Aliyah continued. "My mom. She didn't post bail. I mean. She couldn't." Aliyah looked at her uncle, who nodded.

"Aliyah is a very good student," I piped up, unable to help myself. "She can—"

"I'm gonna get you out of here," Maltese cut me off, putting me in my place.

Message received. If Agent Flynn knew I'd spoken, he'd probably be angry. But I was suddenly tired of playing by the rules. There were no rules here. We were all being held hostage by a killer, and I wasn't going to be silent.

"Why are you here, Uncle?" Aliyah gestured around the lobby.

"This is no place for you," Maltese said, ignoring the question. "I want her released." Maltese looked at Cunningham.

The FBI agent, Flynn, had prepared us for this.

"I don't mind it here," she said. "The people are nice to me. Miss P is a great teacher. I'm learning a lot."

Cunningham said nothing. She stood nearby watching and nodding, as if it were a regular occurrence that family members with explosives talked to each other in the jail lobby.

"Like today, Uncle," Aliyah said. "We read this poem. It was about this man. And it was a short poem, but I liked it. This man, he was swimming in the ocean and waving his arms around. And the people watching on the shore thought he was waving at them. But you know what, Uncle? He wasn't. He was drowning."

My eyes grew wet. The skin on my arms turned to gooseflesh, as it often does when I'm moved by my students. Aliyah wasn't following Flynn's script. She was writing her own.

No one said anything. I tried to hold back the tears. Cunningham exhaled softly.

I watched Maltese. Was it my imagination, or did he move his finger away from the detonator?

"You know, Uncle, there are a lot of good people in the jail too. They're not all bad. You don't want to hurt anybody, right?"

"Did they tell you to say that? Brainwash you here already?"

"No." Aliyah shook her head. "They told me to say that you haven't hurt anybody yet. And it's true. Why you want to die and blow up everybody?"

"They need to get punished." Maltese's index finger moved back, closer to the detonator. "This isn't a good place, Aliyah. It's no place for you. But bad things happen inside the jail. No one cares."

"Did something bad happen to you, Uncle?" Aliyah asked.

Maltese shook his head. "No. Not to me. To Sal." His voice faded.

"Your friend, Sal, the one who died?" Aliyah asked.

Maltese didn't answer.

The jail was absolutely silent. No people coming in or out. No deputies asking for identification. You could have heard a pin drop.

"What happened to Sal, Uncle?"

Though she didn't need any encouragement from me, I squeezed Aliyah's hand.

"They killed him," Maltese said, shaking his head.

I looked at Cunningham. She shook puzzled and shook her head no ever so slightly.

"I thought he died in the Mission," Aliyah said.

"He did. OD'd. Not his fault," Maltese said. "He was clean when he got here. He was good. You know you can buy drugs just as easily in jail as you can on the street?"

Maltese wasn't wrong. I'd heard this from the women. It seemed to be harder in this direct supervision jail with the deputies in the pods, but not impossible.

"When he got out, he was using again." Maltese shook his head. "They killed him just as if they held a gun to his head and pulled the trigger."

"I know you loved Sal, Uncle," Aliyah said. "Drugs," she shook her head. "I got messed up in them. But I'm clean in here. People are helping me."

"I knew Salvador," Cunningham said. "He was in D pod last spring."

Maltese nodded.

"I remember he died just after getting released," Cunningham said softly. "I heard about that, and I'm sorry. That addiction, it's a hard thing to break. Inside. Outside the jail. It's no one's fault."

My thoughts turned to Jazmyn. I glanced at the door to the suite of offices just off the lobby. Was she in there, feet away from Maltese? She must be.

"That's right, Uncle. No one got me addicted. I did that," Aliyah said.

Maltese didn't respond. He didn't seem quite so edgy, but

he still held himself like a serpent ready to spring up and bite.

"You know who gave him the drugs in here?" Cunningham asked.

Maltese shook his head.

"We can do a sweep of D pod. Keep closer eyes on everybody. Shake down the rooms. That's what we can do. No one else needs to die," Cunningham said.

"Uncle, please. Listen to her," Aliyah pleaded. "You haven't done anything yet. You haven't hurt anybody. This ain't like you. You have options."

"I don't have options. Who told you to say that?" Maltese demanded.

I held my breath.

For several long seconds, no one said anything. No one even breathed.

"Who you talk to? Some cop or somebody tell you to say that?" Maltese was angry.

Aliyah shook her head no.

"It's like that poem, Uncle. The one Miss P. taught." Aliyah looked at me. "You don't have to drown."

I wanted to hug Aliyah and kiss her, but instead I stood still and looked at Maltese.

His finger hovered over the button.

"I want her released. Now." Maltese barked the order at Cunningham.

She held up her hands and nodded. "OK. We can try to arrange that."

Maltese jumped back. He was getting agitated.

This was it. We'd pushed him too far. Maltese was going to kill everyone. Aliyah would walk out of the jail, and the rest of us would be blown to bits.

"I want to talk to them. Aliyah walks out of here now."

"Miss P. comes with me." Aliyah clung to my arm to emphasize her point.

Maltese nodded and looked at me.

"Alright," Cunningham said. "Let's talk to them."

CHAPTER 20

10:44 a.m.

When Ryan leaped into the CU van, everyone was grouped around the radio.

"Flynn?" It was Cunningham.

"Go ahead, Cunningham. I'm here."

Ryan leaned in closer, though the deputy's voice came through loud and clear.

"Mr. Maltese wants to talk to you."

"Roger that."

Ryan's spirits rose. It was Maltese in the lobby. Not a setup. Thank God for small miracles. He wanted desperately to ask what was happening with Charlotte and Aliyah but couldn't.

"Mr. Maltese. This is Jack Flynn with the FBI." Flynn's voice wasn't intimidating, but it was firm and had just the right tone of friendly authority. "I understand you want to talk? I'm very glad to get the opportunity."

Silence.

Ryan watched Flynn take a few breaths. Flynn waited patiently and didn't rush to fill the silence.

"I want my niece released."

The bomber's voice cracked on the word niece.

"We'd like everyone to be safe, including your niece," Flynn said. "There are four hundred and eighty-five people in the jail right now, including staff. All of them have families of their own. You don't want their deaths on your hands. I know you don't, Maltese."

Ryan held his breath, waiting for what came next.

"You haven't hurt anyone," Flynn continued as if Maltese had agreed. "So far this is all a misunderstanding. We know you have some issues with what happened when you were incarcerated. We can talk about that. We can try to make things right, Maltese."

"You can't," he cut in. "You can't bring back the dead."

"No, that we can't do," Flynn agreed.

Ryan looked at Perry. They were on the right trail. Someone close to Maltese must have died in jail, but they didn't find anyone recently who died in custody. It was still a piece missing. Then it clicked. Four zero six. Those weren't the first three digits of Maltese's jail number. They were those of the person he'd lost.

Ryan grabbed a pen and a post-it.

406—jail number of someone Maltese knew. Not his.

Flynn nodded.

"I know what it's like to lose someone you love. And I'm truly sorry for your loss," Flynn said.

"Let me try to help you so we can deal with things before anyone get hurt. I know you don't want to hurt innocent people, including your own family. Your sister. She's on her way here too to talk to you. I understand you have nephews too. If you go through with this, they'll have to live with what you've done. How is that going to feel for them? I know you don't want to hurt anyone you love."

Ryan nodded. Flynn was good. Convincing.

Though Ryan's heart constricted when Flynn talked about hurting those you love. Did he love Charlotte? Was he attracted to her? Absolutely. Did he want her? Yes. Did he love her? Ryan's heart said yes.

"I want to make them pay for what they did to Sal." Maltese's voice cut through Ryan's thoughts.

"I understand," Flynn said, gesturing with his hand in a way that said, find out who this Sal is.

"It's a natural reaction when you're hurt, when you're grieving. It feels like if you could make someone pay then that would make Sal's death hurt a little less. But you know that's not true."

Flynn paused to let Maltese absorb his words before continuing. "Sal wouldn't want you to do anything to hurt innocent people or to hurt yourself."

Flynn's voice was calm, reassuring, friendly. It was as if he were in the same room with Maltese, talking to him as if he knew his which he didn't.

This last sentence was a gamble, Ryan thought. The mention of Sal and what he might or might not want could go either way. Would it provoke Maltese?

"Please, Uncle." They could hear Aliyah's voice over the radio. "Listen to this man. He's right. Mama wouldn't want this. Sal wouldn't either. You not this kind of person, Uncle. I know you."

Flynn wisely kept silent.

Seconds ticked by. The only sound through the radio was Aliyah softly pleading with her uncle. Where was Charlotte?

"We can make this easy for you, Maltese," Flynn said.

"You come outside. I'm here. We talk more. You let us help you. No one gets hurt."

"She comes out with me. She walks away. Charges dropped. I don't want nothing on her record."

"Aliyah?" Flynn hesitated for just a second. "OK. We can agree to that."

"Miss P comes too," Aliyah's voice came through the radio.

Ryan exhaled and looked at Flynn. Was Charlotte safer staying in the lobby? Or being used as a human shield by Maltese? Could the snipers get a shot off safely if she did?

"OK," Flynn said.

"You show me the charges are dropped. Then we come out."

The connection went dead.

CHAPTER 21

10:50 a.m.

Aliyah clung to my arm. I wasn't sure that the three of us walking out of the jail together was the best plan. In fact, the odds of us all getting out of here alive seemed to be shrinking.

Was the Sheriff's Department going to comply with Maltese's demand and drop Aliyah's charges? And how soon could that happen? Though I didn't know the process, I imagined they'd have to go to the DA's office. We didn't have that kind of time.

Seconds ticked by. Minutes.

It had been too long. Maltese shifted his weight from one foot to the other. He was growing impatient.

Aliyah hadn't moved from my side, but even she seemed to be getting weary, as she leaned into me.

And what would happen when we walked out of here? Would an itchy-fingered sniper mistakenly shoot me on the spot? Would Maltese let Aliyah go and push me in front of him? Probably.

"Cunningham." The walkie-talkie sprang to life on the desk.

"Pick up the radio," Maltese told Cunningham.

Keeping her finger on the talk button, Cunningham held the radio closer to the bomber. "Flynn here. Maltese, I have some news."

I prayed it would be good news, and we'd all walk out of here alive.

"What."

"We've been in in touch with the prosecutor's office. They're willing to drop the charges. It's a first-time offense, but it's going to take some time."

"How much time?"

"A couple of hours, honestly. We're moving as fast as we can. This kind of thing usually takes weeks."

The FBI agent sounded believable, honest, at least to me. I hoped Maltese thought so.

"No."

Aliyah squeezed my arm tighter.

"I give you my word they're working on dropping the charges right now," Flynn said.

"It's alright, Uncle. He'll do what he says," Aliyah said. "You don't have to worry about me. Please, Uncle. Please don't do this anymore." Aliyah started to cry. Her thin shoulders shook with her sobs. It was the first time since the ordeal started that she'd shed tears.

Bone-thin, in her oversized bright orange uniform, Aliyah looked like she was about to break in pieces.

Flynn didn't say a word.

"Alright," Maltese said. "We walk out of here together. 'Liyah goes free. And you drop the charges."

"That's correct," Flynn said.

"Tell them to unlock the door," Maltese said.

Then he turned to Cunningham. "Put that down." He motioned towards the floor.

Maltese gripped the detonator tightly in his hand. One press and we'd be dead.

Cunningham was a few feet away. But there was nothing the deputy could do. To try to take Maltese down would be certain death for us all.

Slowly, Cunningham bent her knees and placed the radio down. Maltese kicked it away. It clattered across the linoleum floor, skittering towards the bathrooms in a way that jangled my already frayed nerves.

A few seconds later, there was a loud buzz as the deputies released the lock on the front door. The metallic sound of the lock snapping open brought with it a sense of freedom.

"The teacher goes first," Maltese said. "'Liyah, you go behind her."

Great. I was the lucky one.

Aliyah clung to me, digging her fingernails into my arm.

She didn't move.

"It's OK, Aliyah. Just follow behind me like your uncle says."

Finally, she unhooked her arm from mine.

I looked at Cunningham for confirmation that this was the right thing to do, but met Maltese's gaze instead. His eyes, visible through his mask, were like two bullet holes.

Would this be the last time I ever walked across the jail lobby? A lump formed in my throat. The tears that I'd been too scared to shed welled in my eyes, but I dared not move a hand to wipe them away.

"Now!" Maltese shouted at me.

My legs felt as weak as limp spaghetti, but I somehow managed to put one foot in front of the other as I slowly made my way twenty-five feet across the lobby to the front door.

"Stop right there." I did as I was told.

Aliyah was right behind me, sandwiched between me and Maltese. I could hear him breathing and turned my head to see him holding up his hand with the detonator.

Aliyah and I were his human shields.

Cunningham hadn't moved from her position near the desk. She wasn't going to risk attacking Maltese from behind when he could so easily blow us up.

"You go first," Maltese said.

I took a deep breath and grabbed the metal handle of the door. I pushed it open. I blinked several times, my eyes unused to the bright sunshine after the artificial light of the jail. I looked up. It was a gorgeous September day with an azure sky. The sun was warm on my face.

I hadn't realized I'd paused to savor these feelings. Would I know such simple pleasures again?

"Move!" Maltese shouted from behind me.

It was awkward moving as a human chain. Aliyah followed close on my heels. Her breath on my neck. I prayed none of us would stumble, causing Maltese to set off the bomb.

After a few feet, I stopped and braced for what would come next. A bullet from a sniper's gun? Could I suddenly bolt off and run down Seventh Street? Or towards Bryant? No.

Instead of running, I looked around.

Dozens of uniformed police, rescue vehicles, squad cars, fire trucks, and ambulances were positioned half a block or more from the jail, giving a wide perimeter in case the bomb should go off. Despite all the law enforcement and rescue vehicles, I'd never felt so exposed—nor so vulnerable and alone.

It was also eerily quiet. At first I didn't understand why, then realized there were no traffic sounds. The 101 Freeway, which ran next to the jail, was deserted. No cars were heading towards the Bay Bridge. No honking horns, no rush of buses. I'd never heard the city so quiet. It was like watching a movie with the sound off.

I stood frozen on the sidewalk. I sensed dozens of eyes watching us. Where was Flynn? Where was Ryan? Were the snipers waiting for a good angle to shoot Maltese? What exactly was the plan?

"You're free now, 'Liyah," Maltese whispered to his niece. "You walk away."

"Miss P. comes with me," she said.

"No," he said.

"I'm not going unless she comes." Aliyah stood firm behind me.

I certainly wasn't going to argue.

Then suddenly, Maltese shoved Aliyah into me. I lost my balance and felt myself pitching forward, but Aliyah grabbed me before I did.

"Go!" Maltese shouted.

We didn't need to be told twice.

Somehow, my legs obeyed. Aliyah and I were running down Bryant Street. I expected to hear an explosion, gunshots, something. But there was nothing. Had Maltese surrendered? If so, why were we running?

We hadn't gotten very far—we'd just passed the loading docks on the side of the jail—when there were shouts.

I pulled Aliyah into an alleyway on the other side of the loading docks. I wasn't sure if we should stay put here or run further down Bryant Street.

But I didn't have to make that decision. In the next moment, the world exploded.

BOOM. An ear-splitting sound cracked the air open. The ground fell out from under my feet. I reached out to Aliyah as we went flying. The last thing I remembered was pain as I slammed into something hard.

CHAPTER 22

11:01 a.m.

There were moments in Detective Ryan's life where a crime scene played out like it does in the movies. He knew instinctively from the hang of a jacket or the way a perpetrator moved that he was concealing a gun and when he was going to reach for it. Other times, when assessing a murder scene, Ryan could picture the criminal's movements, as if he were a movie director, seeing exactly where the murderer stood and what he did next.

But Ryan did not see Maltese trigger the small detonator in his hand until a millisecond before the explosion. One minute the bomber had his hands up in the air, fingers spread wide as if he was surrendering. The next, he'd touched the detonator, just a fraction of a second before a sniper's bullet split open his forehead.

The roar of the bomb was instantaneous. The shock waves passing under Ryan's feet were far stronger than any earthquake he'd ever felt, knocking him backwards.

His first thought was of Charlotte. He'd seen her run

away from the jail with Aliyah, and it had taken every bit of restraint he had not to shout after her.

Now his second, third, and fourth thoughts were that he had to get to her. Immediately.

Chaos erupted. Sirens. Shouts. Car alarms. Where it had been sunny a moment before, the air was brown and yellow, filled with a thick dust and pulverized concrete. A sharp, metallic chemical scent assaulted Ryan's nose.

His ears rang with a high-pitched sound. Ryan heard commands and shouts as if he were underwater.

He was on his feet immediately, heading across Bryant Street, where he'd last seen Charlotte. Had she known the bomb was about to go off and taken cover?

All around him, first responders, firefighters, paramedics, and police rushed to the site of the blast, where a fire burned.

Through the smoke, Ryan could barely see that the jail was still standing. But how far did the damage extend? Into the lobby? And to those inside? Deputy Cunningham? Jazmyn and the jail staff?

Maltese had been on the sidewalk, not even ten feet from the jail lobby, when he'd detonated the bomb.

Ryan raced across the street heading for where he'd last seen Charlotte, ignoring shouts from Flynn. As he crossed Bryant Street, the enormous Hall of Justice rose before him. Aside from the several windows that had been blown out from the explosion, it looked unscathed. Nothing could take down that enormous cement block of a building, he thought.

Shards of glass crunched under Ryan's feet.

The air was heavy and hot from the explosives.

Where was Charlotte?

"Charlotte!" he shouted, his words barely audible above

the chaos of noise. He choked on the heavy air. A bitter, metallic taste filled his mouth.

"Charlotte!"

Where was she?

Wiping away the dust and sweat from his brow, Ryan pushed on. The Hall stretched almost an entire city block. As he searched near the building, he prayed he'd see Charlotte and Aliyah crouching against its walls. But they were nowhere to be found. It was as if they'd disappeared into thin air.

Ryan needed to find Charlotte. He ran closer to the jail.

Sirens screeched around him. Someone shouted his name. It was Perry. His partner.

He ignored her.

Then he spotted something. Two women, one wearing bright orange, were in the small alleyway just off the Hall. One of them was lying on the ground. The other, the one in orange, was leaning over her.

Even from a distance of several yards, Ryan could see Charlotte wasn't moving.

ELLIE COULD SEE nothing but smoke. She and Sergio had gotten as far as the intersection at Ninth and Bryant, two blocks from the jail, which wasn't that close. Yet even from this distance, the air was full of smoke in various shades of gray and brown.

Ellie realized she was still clinging tightly to Sergio. Just as the bomb went off, he'd grabbed her and tucked her into his big bear of a body to shield her.

She pulled away now, thankful for his quick reflexes. They were safe. Car alarms were screeching everywhere.

Emergency sirens added to the noise. Ellie breathed in the scent of something burning, a chemical smell that came from the direction of the jail.

She clutched her stomach, feeling sick. Was Charlotte alright? Were there any casualties? Ellie looked at Sergio, who stood stoically next to her, his expression grim.

"Do you think...?" Ellie couldn't finish her question.

Sergio shook his head. "I don't know."

Ellie grabbed Sergio's hand. She wasn't going to be held back any longer. She was a reporter. She needed to be at the scene. This time, no police barricade was going to stop her.

"Come on," she said to Sergio. "Let's go."

CHAPTER 23

11:09 a.m.

Ryan kneeled on the sidewalk next to Charlotte. He took her hand in his. And was relieved to find it was warm. He squeezed it. She didn't respond. Then he brought his face close to Charlotte's, checking on her breathing. He held his own breath until he felt her fluttery exhale on his cheek.

Aliyah sat on the other side of Charlotte. Her long black hair curtained her face.

"Are you alright?" Ryan asked.

Aliyah shook her head no.

"Are you hurt?"

"No." Tears fell from her eyes.

"It's all my fault," she said through her sobs.

"None of this is your fault," Ryan said firmly.

"He's my uncle. He did this." Aliyah looked up and gestured to the destruction all around them.

"Yes, he did." Ryan said. "But you had nothing to do with your uncle's actions. What he did is not a reflection on you.

Do you understand? You couldn't have prevented your uncle from doing what he was going to do." Ryan's voice was thick with emotion.

He meant every word. Someone had told him something similar about his own father long ago. The father who was an embarrassment to him growing up, the father who'd gone to jail and prison, and who Ryan still thought of as a stain he couldn't wash out, despite the fact that he was long dead.

"Is Miss P. OK?" Aliyah asked.

"I think so." He carefully pushed Charlotte's curly hair away from her face and gently examined her head. There was no blood. No sign of a head wound. That was good.

Then, he tenderly traced his fingers across Charlotte's cheek. She stirred.

Ryan stood up and shouted for an EMT, waving his arms like a madman. "Over here! Help. We need help over here."

A paramedic spotted him and came running towards them with her medical bag.

"Hang on, Charlotte. Help is on its way." Ryan almost added sweetheart, but caught himself.

He was still holding Charlotte's hand when he felt her squeeze his fingers. She opened her eyes. Her green eyes found his, and she smiled. Then she tried to sit up.

"Easy there." Ryan put his arm underneath Charlotte to brace her just as the paramedic arrived on the scene.

"I'll take it from here," she told Ryan. The medic sat next to Charlotte and began taking her vitals, examining her, and asking questions.

The air was clearing, but the noise hadn't abated. Sirens and shouting came from all directions. How many people were injured, Ryan wondered?

"You sure you're OK?" he asked Aliyah.

"Yeah."

"What you did was very brave," Ryan said. "You helped save a lot of people's lives. Don't forget that."

Aliyah nodded.

When the paramedic was satisfied that Charlotte didn't need to go to the hospital, she turned her attention to Aliyah.

Ryan sat next to Charlotte, holding her as if she might break.

"How many other people ...?"

He shook his head. "We don't know yet."

"Jazmyn? Cunningham? The women?"

Ryan didn't have any answers. He wished he did.

They sat in silence for a few seconds.

"It was so weird," Charlotte said. "Just before the bomb went off, I had this strange feeling. The air was suddenly heavy, and I knew the bomb was going to go off."

The paramedic gave Aliyah the all clear but told Charlotte she wanted her checked out again for any signs of concussion. Ryan nodded. He'd see to it.

Charlotte touched her head. "Good thing I'm hard headed."

"Yes." Ryan smiled. "It is."

"I don't remember really what happened after that," Charlotte said.

"You pushed me in front of you," Aliyah said. "Like you were protecting me."

"Really?"

Aliyah nodded.

Of course, Charlotte would have instinctively tried to save her student, Ryan thought.

Several ambulances had pulled up in front of the Hall,

but Ryan didn't notice if they were full of injured people. His eyes never left Charlotte.

"Let's get you checked out more thoroughly," Ryan told Charlotte, pointing towards the ambulances.

"Alright," she agreed. "Aliyah, you too."

It crossed Ryan's mind that Aliyah could have simply walked away from the scene. She could have gone home, or run away, but she wouldn't leave Charlotte's side. Not even at the price of her own freedom.

Ryan helped Charlotte get to her feet. He kept his arm around her, steadying her.

Feeling her so close to him, Ryan desperately wanted to bend down and kiss her. He wanted to hold her and never let go. He longed to tell her that he'd been a fool for every minute he'd spent apart from her.

But he did none of those things.

Instead, it was Charlotte who made the first move. She reached her hand up around his neck and pulled his face towards hers. Her kiss was electric. Lightning flowed through his veins. He didn't hold back.

When they broke apart, it was Charlotte who spoke first.

"I know you have to go back to work," she told him. "You go. I'm fine. I promise I'll get myself checked out. I'll see you after this is over, remember?" It was what she'd said to him on the walkie-talkie.

"I remember." His voice was husky with emotion.

"You take care of her, too," Ryan told Aliyah. She'd stepped a few feet away when they were kissing, and he appreciated her giving them some semblance of privacy.

"Yup," Aliyah held onto Charlotte.

Then Ryan picked his way through the broken glass and shards of metal all around him. He needed to talk to Perry and Flynn and find out how many casualties there were. He thanked his lucky stars that Charlotte wasn't one of them.

TAKING ADVANTAGE OF THE CHAOS, Ellie pushed her way past the police barricades. She and Sergio were under the 101 Freeway overpass, a block away from the jail. She could see that at least the top of the jail was still standing. The smoke had cleared. But several firetrucks obstructed her view of the building.

"Can you see anything?" Ellie asked Sergio, who was at least a foot taller than she was.

"Not much," Sergio said. "All I see are firetrucks. No ambulances."

That's a positive sign, Ellie thought. Or maybe that's because there are too many casualties beyond the need of first aid? Her thoughts always tended toward the morbid, her family often told her.

Just then, her phone buzzed.

"Ryan." Ellie held her breath.

"She's fine. Charlotte's fine." His voice was thick. "Aliyah too."

"What about other casualties?"

"Don't know yet. But the jail's intact. Most of it. Gotta go."

Ellie's eyes swelled with tears. She reached out and hugged Sergio, burying her face in his chest. He was an enormous bear of a man, with shaggy salt and pepper hair and bushy eyebrows. She knew why Charlotte found him so comforting as a friend.

Sergio hugged Ellie back. Then he asked, "Is she...?"

"She's alive. Charlotte's OK."

Ellie couldn't say why she was crying. Relief. Thankfulness. A reaction to strong emotions of this very long morning.

Sergio didn't move away, even when Ellie knew her tears were soaking his shirt.

Finally, she stepped away and called Helen. Charlotte's sister broke into sobs as she told her Charlotte was fine. She heard George in the background suddenly screeching as his mother cried.

Enjoy them when they're this little and easy to comfort, she felt like telling Helen. But she said no such thing. Instead, she told Helen she had to go.

The crisis at the jail is over, Ellie texted Max. *I'm OK. Probably working late, but see you later at home. Love you to the moon and back.*

Ellie smiled as Max hearted her last text.

Then she turned on her voice memo app, and did what she did best. She got to work recording her impressions of the scene. She'd make Bates proud yet.

CHAPTER 24

Later that afternoon

I had no idea what time it was, but it felt like hours since Maltese set off the bomb. I'd thought of trying to make my way back into the jail to see if everyone was alright. Was Cunningham alive? Jazmyn? My students? Will, the new teacher, who was supposed to start today? I thought again of how most people in the world wanted to stay out of jail. My heart wanted nothing more than to return. Today and every day.

After another medic pronounced me concussion-free, Aliyah and I were escorted to a van to be questioned. I got to meet Agent Flynn, who looked exactly as I'd pictured him: square-jawed, closely shaved head, steely eyed. But kind.

Though I repeatedly asked if everyone was alive, I was only told that the jail had withstood the blast—for the most part. While I was glad to hear that, I cared only about the structure if it meant the people I loved were safe on the inside.

After questioning, Aliyah must have been taken back to

jail, because when I looked for her, she was gone. There were so many members of the Sheriff's Department swarming around, a captain or assistant captain who talked to me for a while too, and whom I asked about Aliyah.

Apparently, her charges weren't being dropped. I only hoped I'd see her soon enough back in my classroom—if I still had a class.

By the time I was allowed to leave, it was late afternoon. I was hungry, exhausted, and wanted nothing more than to lie in a dark room, hoping that my head would stop throbbing. I hadn't been truthful when I told the paramedics it didn't hurt.

Ryan had arranged for a uniformed policewoman to take me home, but before I left, two people swarmed me. Sergio and Ellie both hugged me at the same time.

"My Charlotte," Sergio said. "Thank God you are safe."

"Ditto," Ellie said.

"Were there any other..." Suddenly, I was finding it difficult to find the word that meant people who were killed. It remained out of reach in my brain. I

"Casualties?" Ellie supplied it for me. "No. Just Maltese."

At this news, the tears that hadn't yet come flowed. My arms turned to gooseflesh, and I buried my face in Sergio's chest.

Then Ellie handed me tissues from her purse. Sergio offered to drive me home, but was told by the policewoman who was waiting that I needed to go with her.

Then Sergio insisted on giving me his phone. Mine was in the jail where I couldn't retrieve it. Ellie let me know that Helen had called. She'd told my sister I was safe. Helen was on her way, she'd said, to be there when I got home.

Home. The word had never evoked such pleasure. I'd see Helen and George. The Busters. It felt like days, not hours ago, that I was getting ready for work. No lesson plan could have prepared me for what would happen this day.

Two weeks later

The green and maroon couches in the lobby of the jail were gone. Now the taxpayers would have nothing to complain about.

Taking the place of the sofas, hard-backed bright orange plastic chairs, the same kind the students used in my classroom, ringed the lobby.

The jail had a new front door, equipped with a buzzer and intercom system. For the first time, there was also a metal detector, and a deputy stationed next to it, who searched my book bag when I entered.

Inside, my office had changed as well. There was only one desk now. Not two.

I was still getting used to all the space.

I put my bag down in the empty spot where Jazmyn's desk used to be. Then I walked down the hall towards the copier and the other offices.

"How's it hanging, sista?" Jazmyn asked when I stepped into her new office. Her smoker's voice was gravelly as ever, even more so after the bomb, I thought.

"It's hanging," I said.

The suite of offices had been damaged during the explosion. And there had been another casualty besides Maltese. Will, the new teacher I'd hired, had suffered a heart attack. He was recovering, but his short-lived teaching career was over before it started.

I'd have to go through the process of trying to hire

someone new and wondered if I'd ever get the new charter school off the ground. But there would be time. There would be a new first day of school yet.

Helen and George had come to my apartment every day, bringing food and making sure I rested. The iciness that had existed between my sister and I had melted. Neither of us spoke of it, and I knew at some point we'd have to, but I basked in the joy of having my nephew and my sister back in my life.

Aliyah's mother posted bail for her, and she was no longer incarcerated. I missed her in my classroom, but was glad that she was out. She'd given me her address, and I promised to write to her.

Maltese's full story came out. He had been involved with Sal for years. He was clean when Maltese met him, but started using fentanyl again while in jail. Maltese and Sal were briefly incarcerated at the same time. Maltese saw how easy it was for Sal to get drugs.

After Sal was released, he OD'd. Maltese blamed the deputies, the jail, the other inmates who'd supplied him. The only good to come of the bomb was an investigation that uncovered how drugs had been getting into D pod and put a stop to it. There was a new crackdown on the men's side of the jail and a new counselor hired to lead a drug program like the women's.

After saying goodbye to Jazymn, I headed upstairs to where the women were waiting for me.

I was thrilled to see Cunningham, the movement deputy on duty, waiting with the women. The women were asking questions about their new favorite subject: How had the deputy managed to unlock the offices and get everyone to safety before the bomb went off? Cunningham had never told this story, of course. But news travels faster than any internet speed in the jail, and the women knew what she'd done.

"How's the new man, Miss P.?" Erika asked when I entered.

I blushed. Of course, I'd never said a word about a new man in my life. Sharing personal information was against jail rules. But Erika somehow knew.

True to his word, Ryan came to my apartment the night of the explosion. It was almost midnight when he'd arrived.

When he stood in my doorway, he drank me in with his eyes. Without a word, I led him to my bedroom. We began making love, softly and slowly at first, then more urgently as his mouth caressed every inch of my skin.

"Today we're going to start a new lesson on Romantic poetry." I ignored Erika's question and tried to focus on today's lesson.

"Oohhh. You do have a new man, Miss. P. She all romantic and stuff," Erika said.

The women laughed, as did Cunningham before she left.

I explained that the term Romantic applied to a group of poets in the nineteenth century who rebelled against the more formal rules of the poets before them. And yes, what Erika said was correct. The Romantic poets focused on emotions, especially on love and loss, and strong feelings that nature provoked.

Today we were reading one of my favorite Romantic poets, Elizabeth Barrett Browning. I passed out her Sonnet 43, a passionate love poem to her husband, Robert Browning, every word of which I knew by heart.

This time, I didn't ask for volunteers to read, but dove right in myself.

. . .

How do I love thee? Let me count the ways.
    I love thee to the depth and breadth and height
    My soul can reach, when feeling out of sight
    For the ends of being and ideal grace.
    I love thee to the level of every day's
    Most quiet need, by sun and candle-light.

I continued reading the lines I loved and knew by heart. They'd taken on new meaning now that I had someone to share them with. I'd be sure to quote them to Ryan tonight. I smiled at the thought.

BIBLIOGRAPHY

Poems Charlotte taught in her classroom
   Stevie Smith, *Selected Poems*
   Elizabeth Barrett Browning, "How Do I Love Thee?"
(Sonnet 43)

ACKNOWLEDGMENTS

This mystery novel, like the previous two in the series, grew out of the eight years I spent teaching women at the San Francisco County Jail. Thanks are due first to the many women I had the pleasure of spending time with in the classroom. Though all the characters in this novel are the work of my imagination, the women in the jail taught me about their lives, and I hope I've captured some of the real difficulties these women face both inside and outside the criminal justice system. Any mistakes about this system are my own.

A shout out to my family, Scott and Gus, for their love, support, good humor, and amazing culinary skills. I got lucky. Thanks also to my sister Stephanie Nelson, who read and commented on an early draft and who's been my first reader since about the fifth grade. And to my editor, Kristen Tate at the Blue Garret, for helping make this a better book, and for encouraging the mystery series when I wasn't sure anyone would be interested in reading about women in jail.

I'm indebted to Jane Hammons for years of friendship, support of Charlotte and this book, and for sharing her wisdom about the ups and downs of the writing life with me. I couldn't do it without you.

Finally, I'm grateful to the readers who read the first Charlotte book, asked for another one, and who kindly recommend my books to their friends and families. This book is for you.

If you enjoyed this book, or any of the others in the jail mystery series, would you please leave a review wherever you buy your books? It helps others find my work, and I would so appreciate it.

ABOUT THE AUTHOR

Christina Boufis is the author of a jail mystery series set in San Francisco. The series stars perhaps one of the first Greek-American amateur sleuths—a teacher at a jail who has a knack for finding trouble and dead bodies.

Coincidentally, like her character, Christina is a former academic with a PhD in Victorian literature and Women's Studies who spent nearly eight years teaching women in the San Francisco County Jail. Unlike her sleuth, she has never found a dead body.

As C.B. Peterson, she writes domestic thrillers. Her mystery short stories have appeared in several magazines, including *Pulphouse Fiction Magazine, Rock and a Hard Place*, as well as the anthology, *Larceny & Last Chances.*

She is the co-author, along with Victoria Olsen, of *Some Dark Force, a Victorian thriller*. The novel is the first in a series starring an unlikely band of women detectives. Find more at www.somedarkforce.com.

She lives in Alameda, California with her family and an ever growing collection of animals who wander into the backyard and somehow take up permanent residence.

You can find her at christinaboufis.com. If you join her mailing list, she promises not to send you more than the occasional newsletter.